DEATH AND A DUET

MUSICAL MAYHEM BOOK 2

KM JACKWAYS

OLD SOULS PRESS

Copyright page

Copyright © Old Souls Press 2023

This book is copyright. Apart from any fair dealing for the purpose of private study, research, criticism or review, as permitted under the Copyright Act 1994, no part may be reproduced by any process without the permission of the publisher.

A catalogue record for this book is available from the National Library of New Zealand.

ISBN [978-0-473-68972-8] (ebook)

[978-0-473-68970-4] (paperback)

[978-0-473-68971-1] (hardback)

[978-0-473-68973-5] (kindle)

Cover by Jacqueline Sweet

CHAPTER 1

*I*f you weren't *aware* of these things, the sound could have been the crackling of the fire or the scrape and sizzle of food cooking. It could easily have been the clink of wine glasses or the grate of a knife on crockery. But Esther recognised the tiny laugh and leaned down to snatch her handbag off the floor just as her house keys slipped out.

She grabbed for the keychain with her other hand and managed to wrestle it out of the bright blue hands of the — what was it? A pixie? A fairy? It was shorter than a pencil and almost as skinny, with long arms. It stopped, cheekily, just beyond her arm's reach, then ran off towards the kitchen.

Esther sat up, somewhat flustered, trying not to meet the eye of anyone else at the table. It was the annual

Twelfth Night Feast, held at their local coffee haunt, Grounds for Divorce. Esther had asked Clark to join her and her closest friends for the five-course banquet. She had been to the event for the first time last January, thinking it was just a quirk of their little town. But the tradition had more meaning behind it this year, now that she knew that it was run by the coven who protected Ledstow.

She was still surprised every time she noticed a magical creature. They were often at the edges of her vision, so quick and so improbable that she'd swear that she had made them up to illuminate her otherwise ordinary life.

"All going ok over here?" Lottie asked, coming up to the table, a tea towel in hand. An outspoken character who had fulfilled a lifelong dream by opening the café after splitting up with her husband, Lottie put her hand on her hip and smiled at them.

Esther eyed her. Lottie was also an elder witch in the town coven. She always had a ready smile for them, although it didn't quite reach her eyes tonight. How was Lottie always so calm, even when pixies were causing mayhem in her restaurant?

"Amazing, thanks." Aria answered, dabbing at her lips with her napkin. "I think you've topped last year's feast."

Clark nodded and reached for his pint of beer. Esther had gotten to know the policeman during a murder investigation just a few weeks ago, before Christmas. Since then, they had chatted on the phone or exchanged messages most days, working through what they had found out during the investigation. She still had trouble coming to terms with the fact that someone she worked with had lied to her, and the fact that they had narrowly escaped her grandmother being attacked by one of her co-workers.

"I just had to loosen my belt," Ashton said, covering a yawn. The combined effects of food and the heat from the fire were making them sleepy.

Lottie turned to Esther. "Good, good. And you, sweetie?"

Esther raised her eyebrows, meaningfully. "The food was perfect. But you've got a bit of a *rodent problem*."

The light of understanding sparked in Lottie's eyes and they flicked towards the kitchens. "Well, it is that time of the year," she said, cryptically. "But I'll see what I can do." She hurried off.

"Rodent problem?" Clark frowned. "I'm not sure if we should be—"

"Don't worry," Esther said quickly. "She knows what I mean." At least, she hoped that Lottie knew what she meant. The people in the restaurant were too sober to be seeing pixies just yet.

With a look at the clock, Ashton straightened up. "Come on. We better wake ourselves up. It's almost time."

"It is, too."

"What for?" asked Clark. He was wearing a dark blue shirt, open at the neck and the colour set off his eyes. Esther had decided not to tell him too much about the events of the night and let him experience it for himself. That was the best way to experience Twelfth Night in Ledstow.

Right on cue, Lottie came out of the kitchen with a pan in one hand and a wooden spoon in the other.

Clark leaned in close. "Are you all having me on?"

"Fill your cups, everyone," Lottie called.

Esther poured wine from the jug in the middle of the table into their cups. She lifted hers and waited for the others to clink their cups to hers. The spice smell surrounded her as she brought the drink to her lips.

Ashton stood up, walked unhurriedly over to the sofa next to the fireplace and reached for his guitar, which was leaning against the arm. He lifted the instrument and idly strummed a few chords. The other people in the café started to sing the wassailing song, as if they'd been waiting for a sign.

Esther felt the wine hit her veins and warm up her limbs. She joined in. Some of the staff members banged pots in rhythm. A line of people formed and danced towards the door, some pausing to get their jackets and scarves on. Sarah Harman from the bakery got up and grabbed her walking stick.

Ashton kept the song going. He would wait until the last of the customers got out of their seat, then join them.

"What are we doing now?" Clark asked from behind her.

"Wassailing," she said, joining the end of the train. "Get your coat on."

They left the warmth of the café for the chill night.

"Don't tell me you've never wassailed before?" she said to him, as they spilled onto the street. The sports field opposite them was tipped with frost. "You haven't lived."

"Seems I haven't," he said.

At the corner, they crossed the road and went through the town square.

"More noise, please," Lottie called.

They passed under the stone archway and followed the paved path beneath the ruins of the historic town walls. The iron gates to the allotment were standing open. Dark tree shapes loomed over them. Esther couldn't see much until a lighter flame appeared and a candle wick was touched to it. Lottie held the candle up high.

They were standing in a space between a small orchard and some raised beds surrounded in roughly cut timber. Plants ran wild, sprouting in all directions, over the edges of the beds and trailing onto the path.

A shout came from down the line. "Has somebody brought the wine?"

Esther thought this said a lot about the group's priorities, considering it was freezing cold and dark in the garden. But there was a cheer. Somebody must have indeed brought the wine.

"Watch your step, people."

Esther held her candle up to light it from the first one. The song started up again and Lottie encouraged them to sing louder by banging her pan.

"Waes hail!" she cried.

"Drink hail!"

"Shuffle up, everyone," Lottie called. Ashton was on her left and Clark was on her right. His arm was just touching hers.

Clark elbowed her then. "Do you do this often?"

She threw her head back and laughed, feeling warmth come into her cheeks.

"Only once a year. It's an old custom that brings luck and good harvest to the trees and plants. By lighting fires and bringing joy, the trees awaken from their winter slumber and the sap slowly begins to rise. What do you think?"

"Fascinating," he said. "And what's in this wine?"

"It's actually a hot cider mixed with spices. And it probably has more sherry in it than my nan's Christmas pudding."

"It's a bit different having this in the allotment this time," Aria said. "But it still works."

"Last year, we walked up to the orchard," Esther explained. "But Lottie wanted to make it more accessible."

"Just because we've always done things one way, that doesn't mean we can't make changes that mean these things are welcoming for everyone." Lottie said comfortably, as she sidled past, making sure everyone had made it into the garden and were standing together in a huddle.

"Too right," Clark said, in what Esther had come to recognise was his special local policeman voice. "Don't the locals complain about all the noise?"

"They can try. Send them to me, love." Lottie spoke over her shoulder as she made her way to a spot beside an apple tree that loomed out of the darkness.

"I don't think the people here mind, because they believe in the tradition," Esther murmured. "It's the way it's always been done. And it's only for one night of the year."

Twelfth Night was the fifth of January. It was a traditional night of feasting and revelry, when a peasant could be treated like a king. But it was celebrated a little differently here in Ledstow.

The beat of the makeshift drums increased in tempo and people sang louder. The power of the shared energy and the vibration of her eardrums gave her a thrill and set the hairs on her arms on end. Esther felt something link her to those around her, a gentle touch at the top of her spine. But it didn't take a music witch to know that this was something special.

"Quiet down for just a moment, please." Lottie put her hand up.

Ashton raised his voice. "Oy. Shut it!" A hush fell over the group, until only the shuffling and stamping of feet to warm them up could be heard.

"Kind people, I'll make this brief," Lottie said, and a few people whooped. "Alright, alright. It's down to all of you that we've got such an awesome town full of amazing people. That's it, friends. Thank you all for helping to make Ledstow what it is. Here's to another year of plenty! Raise your glasses." Those who had drinks drank them and the others just cheered.

"The more clatter the better!" Lottie called, banging her spoon against her pan above her head.

The group was even louder on the walk back to the café. The louder everyone else talked, the more Esther had to raise her voice to be heard. She found that she didn't really care.

Somehow, she'd ended up arm in arm with Clark, and she put her leg in front of his to do the walk made famous by The Monkees. Belatedly, she realised she should have communicated the plan first. It went great for one shining moment of synchronicity. Then they went down in a tumble of limbs. She ended up sitting down hard on the footpath.

Clark leaned down to help her up. His face was very close to hers, and his eyes softened, and flicked to her mouth. She remembered how soft his lips were. The air between them sizzled and the gap closed. Their lips touched.

In that moment, a scream rent the air. She froze, and stared at Clark, who stared back. It went on for too long, drilling into her mind, piercing her eardrums. This wasn't someone just getting a fright.

She turned her head towards the sound. It seemed to come from the other end of Ledstow. A woman, she thought.

Esther grasped Clark's hand, quite happy not to be alone. When she was standing up, he put a warm arm around her shoulders.

The others were clustered in groups in the street, suddenly sober. Aria and Ashton caught up to them, their faces blank and eyes wide.

"What was that?"

She shrugged, and a shiver passed over her. "I'm not sure, but I'm not in the mood to find out."

"Are you not coming back to the café? You'll miss the best part," Aria said. "We can warm up again."

"I don't think it's a night to be out," Clark said, and Esther nodded in agreement.

"I have to go back in and get my guitar, anyway," Ashton said. "Might have a quick pint. See you later. Don't do anything I wouldn't do."

"I'll see you tomorrow," Aria said, giving Esther a quick hug.

It was only a few streets to her house, but she was glad of the solid presence of the policeman next to her. Clark was quiet and thoughtful as they crossed the stone bridge and she heard the rushing river to either side, hidden by the darkness.

Around the corner from home, she heard a familiar rasping, like a rusty hinge. She held her arm out for Jay to land on, since the alternative was her head. Or Clark's. And she remembered how that had ended last time.

"It's alright, birdie," she said, when the bird's pinching feet landed on her coat sleeve, although she wasn't entirely sure if it was. The warmth of the alcohol had turned to ice in her veins. There was more than a little mayhem in the air tonight.

Jay took off again and landed on the neighbour's fence.

"That's your bird? Is it allowed to fly free?"

"I can't really stop him," she said. "Jay does what Jay wants."

She unlocked the door to her flat. Jay flew in the door when she opened it and sat on his perch on the bookshelves, head on the side, one eye fixed on Clark.

"Well, have a good sleep," Clark said, trying not to meet the bird's gaze.

"You too."

Once she shut the door, Jay ruffled his feathers out and began preening himself.

"What was that about? Why are you so happy with yourself?" she murmured.

The bird had never seemed to have a problem with Clark before. Jay used to be her grandmother's familiar many years ago. Was he spying for her? Was he simply old-fashioned and prudish?

Esther shook her head. That was just what she needed; a bird that decided it was going to be her chaperone.

She went into the bathroom to wash off her makeup and brush her hair, then got into her pyjamas. Louis jumped up onto the bed and began kneading at her blankets, his claws getting stuck in the threads.

"Hello, kitty. Why are you so needy tonight?" she asked him, only a little annoyed that he couldn't appreciate her pun. "Did you get scared by the noise too?"

The silver kitten brushed its face along the blankets. Hurry up, he seemed to say. She stroked his fluffy back.

"What about you? Do you see magical creatures and ghosties too?"

He paused for an instant, looking into the air behind her, and Esther struggled to keep from turning around to check. *There is nothing there*, she reassured herself. Her scary guard bird would surely warn her, if there was. She slipped her cold feet under the blankets and turned out the light.

When she thought about the sound, tucked up warm in bed, Esther decided it was a shriek, rather than a scream, that they had heard. Otherworldly. Another shiver ran over her as she wondered what in her beloved Ledstow could cause a sound like that.

Waking late, after a disturbed sleep — in which she was sure she had seen Jay perched on the pillow a few inches from her face at one point — Esther got up and threw her clothes on. It was a quick walk down the high street, past bright planter boxes and colourful buildings with sloped roofs, to Grounds for Divorce, which was nestled in between the florist and the antique shop, on the main street of town.

The rich smell of coffee hit Esther's nose as she pushed the heavy door open and stepped into the warmth. She hugged Aria, who was waiting just inside, and looked around with dismay at the number of people who were waiting for their caffeine fix.

"I just got here," her friend said. "Come on. Let's see if

we can get a table. I'd even perch on the end of someone else's, if I have to."

The café was back to normal, with its cute tablecloths and hanging plants and no sign of last night's ribbons and banners. *Almost like magic*, Esther thought.

The line of people waiting was nearly out the door. It seemed that this place was getting busier and busier. She walked past the queue and found a little table near the window.

Esther took off her coat and gloves. "This'll do."

"Did you sleep much?" Aria asked. Her face could have been an advertisement for foundation, with that honeydew complexion and those clear eyes.

Esther shook her head. "I think I finally got to sleep at around one. I started thinking about what I'm doing with my life." She leaned back. The bustle and chatter of people living ordinary lives around her was comforting.

"Oh no," Aria said, familiar with her friend's ruminations. "Do you have any resolutions for the new year, then?" she asked. "We're only a week in, so far."

"Intentions," Esther whispered, leaning in. "Intentions are how we direct our energy," she said. "Witches, I mean. My grandmother is teaching me."

Aria raised her eyebrows. "Cool. You seem to have taken this whole witchy thing on board. I'd be demanding answers if I discovered I had magic at thirty years old. I'd be having a full on tantrum."

Esther laughed. "That's not really my style. The more I think about it, the more I realise that it was always woven through my childhood. My grandmother somehow fostered a love for the unexplained, without ever telling me about witches or magical creatures. She led me to question everything. On some level, I think I always knew I was one."

"Did you, really? Good old Hope." Aria shook her head.

Hope was her grandmother, but to Esther, she was always simply 'nan'. Hope seemed to blame herself for the last murder. She said she should have been more careful with her spells. She had begun teaching Esther what she knew with an almost fervent urgency, although she seemed more and more tired when Esther turned up at the retirement home.

"Yeah, she was a lifesaver when I was younger. Imagine if I'd grown up without knowing her. How different would my life have been?"

"Doesn't bear thinking about. Hey, do you mind ordering me a pot of tea? I've got to go and ring my darling fiancé. He's still acting a bit weird." Aria was already dialling the number as she got up from the table.

Lottie, the barista, smiled when she saw Esther. "How's that cider from last night treating you?"

"I'm alright," she said. "But what about you?"

Lottie's long ash-coloured braid had locks of hair

escaping, as if they were snakes who didn't want to be charmed, and her eyes were ringed in dark grey.

"Oh yeah, I must look an absolute mess. There's drama in the" — Lottie leaned forward — "you know what, ahem, quilting club, at the moment. Some of our members are taking part in the local production and the main actress broke her ankle. It's chaos, I tell you."

Esther cringed. The quilting club was a front for the coven of witches. "Actually breaking a leg, then."

Lottie raised her eyebrows. "Yeah."

"Can't you just— " Wiggling her fingers, she indicated that they should use magic to heal her.

"No, we can't. We keep calm and do it the hard way." From the way she said it, it almost sounded like it was an oft-repeated motto.

Esther wanted to ask more, but now wasn't really the time to get into coven rules and regulations. She lowered her voice. "And how did you get on with our blue friends?"

"Oh, that. I think I may have accidentally left the gate open to them. During the new moon, we normally sprinkle salt on the ground and then sweep it out the door. I must have forgotten it in all the commotion and getting things ready for the big feast. I've been flat out. But it's sorted now."

Esther nodded. "I know what it's like to be lax on the housework. My laundry folding pile seems to grow no matter how much I do." She looked around at the line of people waiting for takeaway coffees. "You're so busy in here today, too. Can I have a latté, a pot of tea, and two pieces of honeycomb cheesecake, thanks?" she asked, tapping her finger on the glass at the chocolate-brown cheesecake that was covered in a frankly improper amount of sweet golden honeycomb.

"Of course." Lottie winked as she reached for a large paper cup from the stack. "Are you and that lovely man getting on alright?"

This was the third or fourth time Lottie had mentioned Clark. Esther felt that it was entirely too many times for the local barista to ask about her love life, even if Lottie was the head of the coven. This very café was where Esther and Clark had first met, and it all seemed a little too coincidental.

"What did you do?" she asked.

"I can't do anything that wasn't going to happen by itself." Lottie laughed. "Perhaps just speed it up a little. So come on, get it moving."

"Did you give him a love spell or something?" she hissed, turning away slightly from the disapproving businessman standing in the line behind her.

"Of course not. I'm deeply offended at the accusation." Lottie turned to the coffee machine, but the edges of her mouth twitched. "Why, did he say the 'L word?'"

Esther narrowed her eyes at the older woman, took

the plates of cheesecake and went back to the table. She took some of the crumb on her fork and savoured it, letting the sweet taste linger on her tongue.

Her phone buzzed. She looked at the message, which was from Clark.

- *Hi. Are you free for lunch today?*

Esther thought back to that moment last night. Her finger traced idly over her lips. She replied that she'd love to, and asked him to choose the place.

Staring out the window, she looked at Ledstow's only half-timbered building, the old market hall, which was now a museum. It was a beautiful building that seemed to lean towards the street.

After a few moments, another message came through. She lifted her eyebrows when she saw that he'd chosen the elegant Hotel Ledstow, which happened to be where Aria worked.

"What's got you all shiny and sparkly-eyed?" Aria asked, pouring herself a cup of tea. "Wait, don't tell me. It's that cop."

"Are you working today?" she asked.

"Yeah, I'm off there after this. Why?"

Esther just smiled, channelling her best Mona Lisa. She decided not to tell Aria that her lunch date was at her work. Aria would see them there soon enough.

"He's adorable, but so serious," Aria said, flicking her fingers at the phone to indicate Clark. "I just want to make silly faces at him 'til he laughs. I suppose he has to be, as a cop, though. Does he have any idea what that horrible shriek was last night?"

Esther shuddered. As a cop. Well, that was only the half of it, wasn't it? What her friend didn't know was that Clark was actually an academic. He was a researcher of parapsychology on secondment as a policeman for a year. He had moved here as many of the reports that he received were concentrated around Ledstow.

"I'll ask him. I'm sure he's looking into it. Anyway, my goals for this year? To play more music and to find a proper job."

Lottie came over with a tray, and placed their drinks on the table.

"What is this 'proper job'?" Aria laughed. "And where can I get one, too?"

"The eternal question," Lottie put in, with a laugh.

"I don't know, to be honest," Esther said. "I know that it's not what I'm currently doing, anyway. You are living your dream, aren't you, Lottie?"

"I'm happy enough," she said, picking up the dirty cups from the next table. "You can't go wrong with unlimited coffee."

"You should look for more gigs. Or make an album

with Ashton!" Aria leaned across the table, her face animated. "That would be so good."

"We don't really have any original songs to make an album," she said. "We mostly play covers."

"Well, maybe you should write some songs."

"Yeah," she said, polishing off her cheesecake. "Anyway, I have to get going. I want to get changed before… "

"Ah, but I really wanted to show you this handbag I'm thinking of buying. You need to tell me if it's too much. When can we catch up again?"

"It's too much," she said, "and I'm sure it'll be sooner than you think. Bye."

She squeezed past a man in overalls, who was complaining to Lottie about the foxes around town.

"They're a nuisance. We can't have our tables outside. They're fearless."

Lottie mouthed, 'help', and Esther threw her a sympathetic look, before sidling past the queue to get to the door.

CLARK WAS WAITING in his police car outside Hotel Ledstow and he got out when he saw her walking up from the bus stop. He wore his black pants and jersey, with his shirt unbuttoned at the throat underneath. He had removed his tie, black bulletproof vest and duty belt. He looked half like a cop, which she supposed was what he was. She was glad that she had changed into her best lambswool sweater and her new boots, as well as a woollen coat overtop and a thick green scarf that Ashton had knitted for her.

Her footsteps crunched on the limestone gravel driveway. The old manor house was sparkling with a recent clean and paint job. Vines, mostly brown at this time of year, crept up the side of the building.

He embraced her and kissed the side of her face, his rough cheek scraping hers. It was friendly and respectful, and Esther tried not to feel disappointed after their sizzling moment last night.

"How have you been? Um, since last night? And aren't you cold?"

Clark opened the heavy wooden door of the old manor. "A bit. Let's get inside. I'm absolutely slammed with work, though. How are you?"

She nodded. "Yeah, I'm good."

"Are you not back at work yet?" he asked. "Two for lunch, please."

"Well, not really," Esther said, as a man asked them to wait for a moment, while he went to check on which tables were free. "My boss at Guitar Pharaoh has decided he's not going on holiday until February, so I only need to do a few shifts. And the shop has been absolutely dead.

Maybe he's trying to give me a bit of a break after what happened with Rochelle. I'm not sure."

Rochelle had recently passed away. Esther and Clark had found out who murdered her. She was the owner of Ledstow's bookshop and the killer had been one of the staff.

"That's nice of him."

The waiter showed them to a table by the window, with a view over the manicured lawns with rhododendrons and azaleas nestled in amongst the oak trees.

"It's unusual. I'm sure he has his reasons. And it seems that Vicky is trying to decide what direction to take with the bookshop. She's been really vague about whether she even wants to continue stocking our music books."

"I heard Ashton saying last night at dinner that the bookshop isn't getting as many customers, either. You'll be at a loose end, then?"

She nodded. "I think word has gotten out about what happened with Rochelle. She really was the driving force behind that bookshop. But having the spare time means I can play my music and read books that I've had sitting on my nightstand for months, though. I'm still cleaning the house for my neighbour, as well."

He rubbed at the stubble on his chin. "Busy morning for me. We had official reports about that scream coming from all over, but most were from one street. I've called a few of the people back this morning. They all report hearing the scream coming from outside, but no one saw anything. We're expecting to hear something about an assault on a female victim pretty soon."

"Oh, that's awful." That scream. It didn't quite sound like a person to her.

Aria was standing by the door to the foyer, dressed in her white blouse with the golden nametag and crisp, black trousers. Her hair was pulled tightly up into a bun now. Esther gave her a little wave.

Their waiter, a young man with blond hair that was also in a bun, came over to them.

"I'm sorry. We haven't even looked yet," she said to the waiter, trying not to glance over at Aria, who was shamelessly making kissing faces at her from the other side of the room.

"It's alright," Clark said. "I'd like the salmon, thanks. You might like the Spanish Garlic Chicken? It's cooked in a white wine sauce and comes with rice and green beans."

"Yes, thanks," she said to the waiter, who nodded once and left them to it. "You checked the menu first?" She shook her head. "Monster."

"Of course."

"And you remembered it word for word?"

"Doesn't everyone?"

She shook her head, then bit her lip, watching him with a mischievous look. "And did you check me out first?"

"Well, yes," he said. "We first met when I was working on the case, remember?"

She let her shoulders droop. "Yeah."

He leaned forward a little and a gleam came into his eye. "I've got something that you might be interested in."

"What is it?"

"Well, you recall about my job?" He lowered his voice. "I mean, my real job?"

She nodded. He was referring to being a Professor of Parapsychology, the study of 'psi' or unexplained mental phenomena, such as telekinesis and telepathy. Knowing that he saw Ledstow as a fantastic research opportunity gave Esther chills, as she'd just discovered she was from a family of musical witches.

"If any emails come in that are slightly out of the ordinary, Shona forwards them to me. And some of them are really out there," he said, pouring her a glass of water from the slender jug and passing it across. "This morning, there was a message that simply said, 'I dreamt of a murder.' That was all. It was from a generic email address and the name at the bottom was 'Rock 'n' Roll 68'. I've replied and said I'd like to hear more about it. It could be a case of precognition, which is when someone dreams of something before it happens. Because it contained the 'M word' and due to the timing coming straight after that scream, I couldn't just delete it without following it up."

"Or it could be someone who had a little too much brandy."

"Yes, there is always that possibility. I do tend to take these things seriously, because precognition would be a big deal in my field."

"Do you get a lot of emails like that?"

He nodded. "Word gets out that I'm investigating paranormal phenomena and I attract all sorts. Interesting characters. Interesting stories. I make sure to deal in research, facts and figures, even though it is not a mainstream science. I try not to engage too much, though, since the incident with the support group." He waved a hand as if that wasn't important and she decided not to ask any questions.

"I see."

"I thought you might be interested as you said your grandmother always discussed the unexplained with you."

"Oh, right. Yes, she does," Esther said, nodding. She busied herself with eating the last of her green beans. It was all a little too close to home. They passed the rest of the meal pleasantly, chatting about other restaurants they'd eaten at around town.

Her handbag buzzed and reached down to grab her phone. It was a message from Aria.

- *Why didn't you tell me? I could have got you the best table and served you myself*

She tapped out a quick reply, smiling to herself.

- *That's precisely why I didn't tell you x.*

"That was a really nice lunch," she said, looking up at Clark, who was watching her.

"It was," he agreed. "I've got a boring afternoon of paperwork to go back to now. And the Head of Department from my university rang this morning just as I was going out. I'll have to call him back."

"Oh?"

"I think Edwards will be wanting to check up on how I'm going. Whether I'm making use of my time here to do some robust research."

"Good luck, then."

Clark stood up and got his wallet out. "I'll pay."

"We'll split it," she said, firmly.

"Alright," he said, tapping his card, "but at least let me give you a ride home. We're on the edge of town here."

"Yes, thanks." In her pocket, her phone buzzed and she looked down at it. "Speak of the devil, and he shall send a text message," she said, with a laugh.

"What's that?"

"Oh, it's just my boss. Turns out he needs me to work for a few hours this afternoon."

"Well, I suppose it's good for the wallet."

"Yeah, it is. He's not too bad, really."

"Shona's not too bad, either, once you get to know her."

"I'll take your word for it," Esther said, lifting her eyebrows, thinking of the police boss's 'bad cop' persona.

Clark opened the door for her and she headed towards the patrol car. "Is this even allowed?" Esther asked, getting a little thrill as they walked towards the bright yellow and blue police car. "For civilians to go in your car?"

"Why not?"

She opened the car door and got in. There was a small picture that she guessed was a photo of his younger sister on the edge of the dashboard. She had short, blue hair cut into a pixie cut and a sweet, crooked smile.

Clark started up the car and drove out of the long driveway that wound slightly downhill through the grounds. Esther was just about to ask him if he was busy next weekend when his radio made a noise.

A crackly voice came over the speaker.

"All units to 19 Beekeeper's Close. That's One Nine. One Nine."

She looked over at Clark, who ran a hand through his hair and turned on his indicator to pull over. "I'm really sorry about this. Don't know why Patrice says all units when it's just the two of us on call," he grumbled. "I think it makes her feel like she's in a big city police department."

"That address is just around the corner from here. It sounds like you have to get there quickly."

"Is it off Schoolmaster's Lane?" he asked.

"Yes. You can just drop me off and I'll walk or catch a bus back."

"Are you sure?"

He slowed as they pulled into the narrow street. It was lined with terraced cottages, which looked to be heritage buildings, so he had to pull over at the start of the street into a small, cobbled area to park. It was one of the loveliest streets in Ledstow.

Esther got out of the car and put her bag strap over her head. Clark came around to her side, still pulling on his jacket.

"Alright, I'll talk to you later, then."

He reached for her hand. "Hey, I'm really sorry about this."

"Don't worry about it. I can find the nearest bus stop. See you later." But she wondered to herself if it would always be like this. Him going off to investigate crimes. On call at any time.

She shook her head. No, he was actually a university

professor. And what was she doing getting ahead of herself anyway?

That little voice was anxiety speaking, she knew. It told her she had to know where she stood. They'd had a few dates and a few good conversations. They were enjoying each other's company. That should be enough for now.

THAT AFTERNOON, Esther watched the young man clean the window of the cheese shop over the road from the window of Guitar Pharaoh. It was a mark of how bored she was that she noticed when he missed a spot.

One customer was staring lovingly at the electric guitars, but Esther knew that she'd never buy anything. Blaine came in here most days in her break. She looked as if she was only about eighteen. Esther privately hoped she'd be able to buy herself a guitar one day soon. Otherwise, the shop was blessedly quiet.

After Esther had paid the monthly invoices, she had nothing more to do, so she reached for *Eleanor Oliphant is Completely Fine*. Soon enough, she became absorbed in the book and only noticed how hungry she was when the bell over the door jingled.

"Afternoon."

"Long time, no see," she said to Clark, immediately standing up straighter.

"Yes. Sorry to barge into your work like this." He cleared his throat. "I needed someone to bounce this off and, well, you did pretty well with the last case."

Esther felt a warm glow. "Have a seat in the staff room. I can keep one eye on the front door from there." She gave herself a mental slap in the face. She was preening like a cat in the sun.

He sat down at the table. "You remember I told you at lunch about that email?"

"Yes. Would you like tea?"

Clark adjusted his glasses. "Yes, please. Well, they declined my offer to meet. But they did say that, in their dream, an actor here in Ledstow was killed. Then, today, when I was called to Beekeeper's Lane, it was because Mr Castle turned up dead."

"Who?" Esther poured some boiling water over the tea in the teapot, inhaling the comforting scent. She got out two cups.

"Mr Castle. Well, not exactly 'turned up dead'. Funny phrase that. I should say that the house I went to on Beekeeper's Lane was his flat. His body was found in the kitchen by his wife."

"Milk?"

"What? Oh, yes, thanks."

She added the milk and brought the tea cup over.

"What happened?"

"He was fifty nine years old. A solicitor. He had been on heart meds. His wife confirmed he's had trouble with his blood pressure in the past. Open and shut case, you would think."

Esther looked down at the table. "Oh no."

Clark eyed the tea cup, as if he didn't quite trust it, before taking a sip. It was decorated in a very dated gold and purple design and had a chip in it. Esther had bought it from the charity shop when her boss sent her to buy some crockery and cutlery for the staffroom.

"I haven't even got to the weirdest part yet," he said. "He's an actor."

Esther frowned. "What else do you know about him?"

"Absolutely nothing yet. Except that Harding Castle is a lawyer here in Ledstow and an actor with the local drama society. So I need to find out more about this dream. I can't tell the Detective about a random email. It's not evidence, as such."

"Not the production here in town? Lottie at the café just told me that someone in the cast broke their ankle."

"Really?"

She nodded. "The main actress. Wait — Harding Castle? That sounds more like a National Heritage site than a person's name."

He eyed her. "You've not heard of him?"

She shook her head. "No, can't say I have. But that

doesn't mean much, unless he is a musician. Was," she corrected herself.

"No, he wasn't," he said. "He was an actor in some of the West End musicals, oh, thirty years ago, I think." He turned the saucer around to look at the design. "I wondered if you could check it out for me? Some of them might know I'm with the bobbies."

"You mean check out the drama society? Ask them questions?"

"Yes. It's likely just a coincidence."

"Hmm. My nan would say that just because we don't see the chain, doesn't mean two things aren't linked. Surely, the person who emailed you is the first port of call?"

He nodded and leaned back in his chair. "Smart lady. I'm going to keep encouraging them to meet with me. It would be a lot easier than getting the resources to track them down. But it's all strange enough to make you take a second glance, isn't it?"

Esther nodded. It was certainly strange. An anonymous warning. An actor, dead. A female scream and a male body.

CHAPTER 3

It was the next morning when Esther knocked on the chipped and faded door of the old stonemasons' hall, peeking in when somebody opened it.

The Ledstow Drama Society was in disarray. People were packing costumes into boxes, and some were sitting around drinking from mugs, looking gloomily at their scripts.

"How can I help?" The person who opened the door was tall with short, black hair. He had tanned and muscled arms and he reached out with both hands to shake hers. He came across as a very gentle man, although the black sweatshirt with torn-off sleeves belied that image.

"It's nice to meet you," he said, with a smile. His eyes were a warm brown beneath long lashes. "I'm Lee. What are you after?" he asked again, in a faintly American accent.

"Well, I'm a... friend of Harding's. I wanted to talk about what happened to him with people who understand."

"Oh," he said, nodding. "Right now? We're practising."

Esther eyed the chaos inside and lifted her eyebrows.

Lee shrugged. "There isn't that much practising going on, it's true. I'll just check for you as we're not supposed to let anyone in." He laid his finger alongside his nose. "Show secrets."

"Okay. Thanks." He strode off, presumably to find someone to ask.

"At least come in a bit. It's cold," a young woman with fair skin said, bundling her inside. "We don't usually use this door," the woman continued, closing the door behind Esther. She sat down on a box and tied her long strawberry blonde hair into a ponytail, and adjusted her headband that was tied in a small bow on top, reminding Esther of ears. "It's the audience door."

"Oh sorry," Esther said.

"There's not much to do today. You've heard the news, I suppose?"

"Yes. Terrible."

"I'm Celia," the woman said, gesturing at her tights. "I'm channelling my character right now. Poppy's my name, really. Lee is lovely but he'll do whatever *she* wants." She rolled her eyes towards Bettina, then walked off, muttering lines to herself.

Esther stuck to the edge of the hall, nervous that someone would call her out as an imposter. But she needn't have worried. Everybody seemed wrapped up in their own problems.

An old man was kneeling on the ground, working on a customwood set piece and it seemed he couldn't quite get it to fit with the other piece, as he kept stopping and saying, "Blast it all!" and "What does a man have to do?" It reminded Esther of putting together flatpack furniture.

The hall itself was small and didn't let in much light. She'd only been in here once or twice at night, so she hadn't really noticed before.

The stage director was a woman with expansive gestures and an Eastern European accent, called Bettina Van Helse. Esther knew this because Clark had given her Bettina's business card. She was walking around the hall, weaving effortlessly between pieces of set, a mobile phone stuck to her ear, speaking in a very loud voice.

"We're a few days out from the dress rehearsal! The show absolutely must go on," Bettina said. "It's for charity." She stared at Esther, as if she was about to argue.

Esther nodded, but Bettina was talking to whoever was on the other end of the line and she marched on.

Another woman, who was tall, with smooth, bright

red hair, streaked with black, went past. She must have been sucking a cough lozenge that smelled of menthol.

"Oh, Helen," Poppy said to her. "You're back. Am I wearing a wig or what?"

"Walk with me," she said, in a hoarse whisper. Esther thought the woman must have a cold. Poppy jumped up and followed her.

Esther looked around. Bettina was making a beeline for her, followed by Lee.

"No visitors. I'm really sorry. Out." Bettina dismissed her with a flick of the wrist and sauntered off. Some people really could make words sound like the opposite of what they meant.

"That's the rules," Lee said, with a shrug. "She's extra stressed because we don't have our two main actors. There was poor Harding and also our leading lady broke her ankle."

"Both of them?" she asked. "Why is there nobody else? Don't the main actors normally have understudies who can step in?"

Lee gave her an appraising look. "The understudies both quit a week ago."

"Couldn't you convince them to stay? How are you going to perform the play?" Esther didn't see how the show could possibly go on. It seemed hopeless.

He shook his head. "No, we couldn't," he said, flatly. "But we will perform the play. We always do."

He turned towards the door again, but Esther was determined to keep him talking.

"Er, what show are you doing?" she asked.

"It's a modernised version of *As You Like It*. Someone from our own club wrote the songs."

"Ooh, I remember that one from high school."

"It's been a lot of fun."

"And was Mr Castle well-liked in the drama club?"

"Of course, yeah." His eyes flicked away from hers. Esther pressed further, asking about the other cast members and their past productions. As the questions went on, Lee stumbled over himself more and more, and went back to revise what he had said. It became obvious that he had been told not to say anything about Harding Castle.

"I thought we told you to leave," Bettina said, from behind her. "We're grieving," she added, putting her hand to her chest and flinging her head back.

♫

"I'VE GOT serious misgivings about that woman," Clark said, when Esther rang him while walking home from the hall. "She sounds like a box of fluffies."

"Everyone else seemed nice. But it was difficult to talk to them."

"I thought it might be. They'll have got a shock about

Mr Castle and they're probably fending off the press too. He was quite well-known in his day."

"Did you get anywhere with the dreamer?"

"Who? Oh, right. Not yet."

"I'll talk to you later," she said.

When she got home, she decided to do some baking. She pulled out her grandmother's recipes for biscuits, and got to work, getting lost in the familiar routine of measuring, sifting and mixing. As she melted the butter, she reflected on whether she should be getting involved in the case. It wasn't her job. She could walk away any time. But if you knew that someone was likely murdered, surely it was your responsibility to find out who did it. Because if you didn't get involved, could you ever live with yourself?

She rolled the dough into little balls, then pressed them with a fork dipped in flour. It was a pity that the drama club was such a closed book. Every time she'd asked a question, they'd turned it around.

She put the two trays into the hot oven, and leaned back against the bench as a sweet, chocolatey smell began to rise up from the baking. She would have to remember to swap them over half way through.

A smile spread across her face. The beginnings of an idea had already seeded in her mind.

A ridiculous idea. An idea that Clark would either scoff at or laugh at.

Esther wondered if other people had these intrusive ideas, then she shook her head. Of course they did. *But they don't act on them, Esther Forte.*

♫

CLARK TURNED up at her flat that afternoon, and Esther wished she'd changed out of her grotty sweatpants and thermal top that she'd thrown on when she got home. She brushed at the cocoa powder that had found its way onto her top. Luckily, he didn't seem to notice.

"Have a seat," she said, gesturing to the dining chair.

"Thanks," he said, distractedly. "Alright, I agree that all the circumstances are fishy enough for a murder to be likely. I've told Shona and she is on board with what I'm doing. She doesn't know that you're involved too. She has given me a few weeks off my normal duties to look into it and prove that there's enough evidence for a murder investigation. I had to offer to work the weekend shifts for a month."

"Oh. That's quite a commitment."

"She'll owe me if I turn out to be right, though. If we turn out to be right."

"Exactly."

He spread out a file on the desk and adjusted his glasses. Whenever he did that, Esther just about melted. She almost missed what he was saying.

"Sorry, what?"

"Here are the notes from where the body was found. Harding Castle was found in his own house by his wife. The body is unscathed. No weapon was found. The doors were locked. It looks exactly like a medical event from the police point of view."

"What do we know about the wife?"

He shook his head. "Police have questioned her. Wendy's her name."

"Wendy Castle? Are you kidding?" She imagined a romantic scene at the ruins of a castle on a moor with a winter breeze whipping her hair. It was like something from a Gothic novel. She waved a hand at his blank look and sighed. "Oh, never mind. Was it you and Shona who questioned her?"

"No, it was Derek. He is pretty good at getting a feel for people, though. I trust Derek."

"Okay, so we've got a man who was a lawyer, and was an actor in his spare time. The doors were locked? No one else lives with him?"

Clark nodded yes to both. "Just the wife. He does have one grown up child who lives out of town," he said.

"Who else had come to the house that day?"

"Well, his wife said that Lee, one of the actors, was going to drop something off to him. I'm not sure if he came or not. Bettina, the producer, was going to give him a lift to rehearsal."

"I met Lee today," she said. "Was there anything else about the kitchen?"

"There were a few dirty dishes in the sink. The rubbish bin contained two crumpled up pieces of paper; one was a brochure about fitness, the other was a newsletter about the village hall." Clark reached over and pulled out a piece of paper from the pile, with a picture printed on it. "Ah yes," he said. "He was wearing pyjama bottoms, see."

Esther thought it over for a moment, as something twigged in the back of her mind. "Wait, he was found around lunchtime by his wife? He was still wearing his pyjamas at that time?"

"Yes."

Esther wondered if he'd died earlier than they thought. "I'm definitely not against pyjama days. Heaven knows I've had enough of them! But it seems a little odd if he had people coming around and he was planning to go to the rehearsal. Doesn't it?"

"Maybe so," Clark said. "Or maybe not. We can't over-think everything."

That's where you're wrong, Esther thought. *I definitely can.* She gave him a nod and smile, but she noted, with satisfaction, that he put a tiny question mark next to 'Time of Death'.

"So, he was a lawyer. Well, that leaves it wide open for people who might have had a motive," she said. "I'll make us a hot drink."

Tea would make him more agreeable to her idea, she was sure. A biscuit or two wouldn't go astray, either.

"Yes. I've asked for a list of the cases he was working on." He picked up his phone. "It is a difficult one because there's no weapon to be found. No visible wound either. Maybe poison?"

"White? Tea, I mean. Have you tried ringing the head of the drama society directly?" she said, carrying a cup and saucer through from the kitchen and placing it on the table in front of him. "In your capacity as a cop, I mean?"

"I'm ahead of you there. Her exact words were: 'Go away, we've already talked to someone. Leave us to grieve in peace.'"

Esther remembered how Bettina had stared at her in that challenging way. "I can believe that. It does sound like the lady in charge."

"Did you bake this?" Clark said, around a mouthful of biscuit. He was holding his phone up to read out what was on the screen. "Alright, I just got an email back from Harding's office. He was a solicitor, so he'd been doing property conveyancing and things like that. Nothing in court, although I suppose he still could have crossed the wrong person in that line of work."

Esther put her teacup down in the saucer carefully. She looked Clark straight in the eye. "I'd like to suggest something. Keep an open mind, eh? Well, you know how all of the evidence points to the drama society having a lot to do with it?"

"Yes, I suppose it does."

"It looks as if we might need to get into character."

"Do you mean the play?" Clark took off his glasses, rubbed his eyes, and sighed. "In an ideal world, we would find out a lot more about everyone involved if we were involved in the play. Yes."

"No, hear me out. I'm serious. The play is a modern, musical version of Shakespeare's *As You Like It*. I can sing passably and act a little, and I do love musicals."

Louis was perched on the edge of the couch, and turned to look at Clark as he reached forward for his cup. He frowned, no doubt remembering the injuries the kitten had incurred on him in the past. "I've never seen a version of the play. Or read it."

Esther waved his argument away with a flick of her wrist. She was becoming more and more convinced that this was a great way to figure out what was really going on in the drama society. If she was honest, she was getting a little excited about taking part as well.

"Well, that's easily remedied. You can sing alright, can't you? And you've already proved that you've got a crazy memory. Between us, we make up one excellent actor."

He smiled. "I think that the more pressing problem is

that we have to work. We can't just take time out from our jobs to focus on this for the next — what — four weeks?"

"I think we can," she said. "You've been absolutely flat out for weeks, so you need a break. I'm not really needed at work right now. Come on, it'll be fun."

"Even if," he paused and shook his head as if he couldn't believe he was asking, "that were true, why would they let us in?"

"They are desperate for people to step in. It's one week until the second dress rehearsal and two weeks until the production starts. Do you remember that Bettina mentioned it's for charity? Think of all the time and money that has already been put into it."

Clark looked her over, thoughtfully, as if examining a new sort of creature; one that he couldn't decide what to do with.

"I could probably swing it with Shona. She knows I'm interested in the case," he said, looking to the side as he considered. "But a professor pretending to be a cop pretending to be an actor? It's ridiculous."

"Yes, it is. But sometimes we all need a little bit of the ridiculous," she said, firmly.

Clark stood up and looked out of the window. After a few minutes, he said: "It's not a bad plan." It sounded as if it was physically painful to admit. "But I should warn you. It could be dangerous. We don't know if whoever killed Harding is going to strike again."

"I think it's probably someone after his money, so they may not necessarily be violent. But I'll get my nan to teach me some…" She paused, unsure of how much she should tell him. "Self defense moves."

He cocked his head to the side. "Why do I get the feeling that you'd probably investigate this even if I didn't agree?"

"I'm not sure," she said, with a grin. "Because I solved that last case pretty much by myself?"

The noise that erupted from Clark could hardly be called a snort; it was so violent. But Esther ignored it.

"'The play's the thing,'" she quoted. It was exciting thinking about being part of a show.

"I hope so," he said.

Esther pushed her advantage. Besides the fun of acting, she had to admit she was looking forward to spending some time working closely with Clark. "So we're going to audition?"

He let out a long breath and his eyes held hers for a long moment. "Fine."

"I was hoping for a little more enthusiasm, but it'll do."

CHAPTER 4

She wasn't lying, Esther told herself. Sometimes you didn't have to tell people everything. Clark would be perfectly happy, thinking they could get the roles on their own merits.

As they had worked through the details of their plan, a niggling feeling that it was full of holes came to her.

Later that day, at home, she couldn't shake it. Too many things could go wrong. She recognised the familiar increase in her heart rate and the clammy hands of anxiety and tried to distract herself by playing the ukulele. But the songs wouldn't come this afternoon. Jay walked back and forth across her windowsill, watching her.

She could muck up the audition. Clark could muck up the audition. He could be recognised as a policeman.

They could accidentally blurt out something about the crime.

Finally, she decided that, instead of sitting at home, playing over all the scenarios in her mind, she'd make a plan for the eventualities. And she knew that her grandmother could help.

♫

HOPE HAD BEEN NAPPING but she was sitting up in the chair when Esther arrived at the retirement home. She opened her eyes as the door creaked open and a smile spread across her face.

"You're glowing, Blue Eyes," she said, using the nickname she'd called Esther since she sang Frank Sinatra at school.

"Am I? Well, I'm using my mind again, nan. That always gets me excited. I'm that much of a nerd." Esther leaned in to hug her grandmother.

"I must be the original nerd, then," Hope said. "I feel like that when I've got a particularly hard Sudoku puzzle to work on."

Esther put a tin of biscuits down on the table and sank into her usual armchair, which was covered in a colourful blanket. "You don't even seem to find them that difficult. I hope you're feeling well?"

When Hope nodded, Esther said, "Good. Because I

need your help. Can you please tell me more about intentions?" she asked.

Her nan's eyes widened. "Well," she began, "we manifest certain outcomes using our energies."

Esther was still thrilled every time she heard her nan talk like this. She sometimes wished they could have had these witchy discussions when she was a little girl, but tried to brush off the regrets.

Her life would have been different if she knew she was a witch, but whether it would have been better or worse was anyone's guess. *Now is as good a time as any*, she thought.

"So we wish really hard. We repeat a phrase. What?"

"No, I wouldn't describe it like either of those. We set a clear picture in our mind of our goal. Similar to visualising, I suppose. You know, you close your eyes and see the ball going into the goal. You picture yourself shaking the boss's hand getting that promotion. Those self-help books have us to thank for some of these ideas. Imagine their faces if they knew." Hope laughed.

"Okay. Then we wave a wand?"

Hope shook her head. "No wands here, sorry. With our musical magic, it's a bit like a puzzle. We sing the notes. I know you studied theory and can speak the language of music. Now you have to use it to create. Maybe I'd have to show you. It's really very hard for me to explain," her nan said, passing a hand across her forehead.

"I think I get it. I felt it a little when I set that ghost free, you know, when I was young. I've remembered the whole thing. I was thinking at the time about the Titanic and listening to the girl play a song. It felt like it wasn't quite finished, so I sung the final note. It was…"

"Like a puzzle, yes. You had an intention and you brought it to life."

"Are there any little self defense spells I could learn?"

"Oh! That's a really good question. I'll have to have a think." Hope put her head on her hand and stared out the window. It went on so long that Esther was sure she had drifted off to sleep.

"Nan?" she said, softly.

"I'm thinking," she said, eyes flicking back to focus on her. "It's not as easy as just flicking off spells, because we were never taught in a magical school or anything. I'm thinking back to any times I've needed to protect myself. Can you imagine how many memories I have to sift through? I've lived such a colourful life. Oh, I wish I'd written it all down in one big tome."

"Oh, that would have been great. But hindsight is 20/20, isn't it?" She reached for the tin. "It must be a good time for some home baking then, while you have a think."

Esther slid her fingers around it to open the top. She

showed the contents to Hope, who wafted the smell towards herself with a rapturous look on her face.

"Oh, yes, please. What have we got here?" Hope asked. "Looks like coconut crunchies and chocolate puffs."

After selecting a coconut biscuit, Hope took a delicate bite.

"My recipe! The taste and smell of this is bringing back a lot of things. Do you know," she said, closing her eyes as she savoured the taste, "that I had to bake biscuits every day growing up?"

Esther took one of the chocolate ones. She had, of course, sampled a few when baking them. "Every day. I can't imagine it. It must have taken you so long."

"It must have. But, you know, we just got used to it. I never would have thought back then that I would become a singer. Never. It was like a dream."

"You've had an amazing life, nan."

Hope nodded. "The thrill of performing in front of a live audience and getting that instant reward is nothing on how it feels to perform with magic. It's something else."

There was a comfortable silence while they were both lost in memory. Esther was remembering when she had played a song with Ashton and her friends had come along to practise and their energy made her perform better than before.

"I wanted to tell you about how it feels to do musical

magic, Blue Eyes. It's like nothing else. There is almost another layer of reality that we reach into and pull magic from. Nothing can be created or destroyed, I know that much, but we can change things, subtly or not. So when I want to do something with my magic, I hold an intention in my mind of the way I want it to be and then sing a finished melody. It's easiest when the change is really small, to start with."

"Alright."

Hope indicated the biscuit that Esther was lifting towards her mouth. "So, start with that biscuit and visualise it in your mind. The chocolatey smell. The texture or mouth feel."

"I'll visualise it popping into my mouth," she said, licking her lips.

"Yes, in a minute. But I want you to think of a crack right down the middle of the biscuit. What would it sound like snapping? How would it feel? And most importantly, how would it look? Have you got that? Now sing it to life."

As strange as it sounded, that made sense to Esther. She closed her eyes and hummed a note. And another. She heard something plop onto the carpet, opened her eyes and found that she was still holding half. She reached down quickly and scooped the other crumbs off the carpet.

Her nan sucked in her breath and clapped her hands together.

"I did it?"

"First pop."

"But how have I been doing this without meaning to?" she asked. "Like in the cemetery? It takes a lot of concentration and focus."

"You must have simply had a picture in your mind of Ledstow in another season. That was why all of the leaves fell off the tree."

"So I don't have some wonderful weather magic that can change seasons?"

"I wouldn't think so. At the beginning, your magic comes in fits and starts. One day, it might be really powerful and the next, nothing. It takes time to control the flow. Like a power surge, almost, if that makes sense."

"So think really hard about the end goal and sing? Easy."

"You have to sing with perfect pitch, too."

"Yup. Got it." Her nan gave her a look, but Esther was excited. Surely, she wouldn't need to use this, right? But if it came to it, she had it there.

"So, why are you suddenly so keen on learning everything I know?" her grandmother asked, with her usual acuity.

"There's been another death here in Ledstow, nan.

And we think it might be a murder, but the police are treating it as a health issue."

"They aren't after us again, are they?"

"No, it's nothing to do with that. It was an actor who died. He'd be rolling in it, I'd say. So it's probably money-motivated. He was a lawyer as well."

"Well, be careful."

"I will," she reassured her grandmother, reaching over to pat her hand.

"Oh, I know. I don't mean that you'll be in danger. You're too smart for that. I mean that people would love to learn our secrets. So magic is always the last recourse. Remember that."

THE NEXT MORNING, Clark gave Esther's hand a quick squeeze as they knocked on the door of the hall.

"Is this absolutely wild? This is foolish, right?" she asked for the tenth time, but the door was already opening.

Bettina stood in the doorway, black beads swinging as she turned to face them.

"Hello. Could we speak to the casting director please?"

"That's me, at this stage." Bettina said. "Almost

everyone else has dropped out. We don't even have understudies."

She beckoned them in, then walked quickly to the end of the hall, issuing commands to other people as they went: "Ring costuming about that." "Try it again but keep your head down." "Can you ask your daughter if she can sell the tickets?"

Esther and Clark exchanged glances, amazed they had even gotten in the door. Bettina must be distracted.

"What happened with the understudies?" Clark asked, and Esther nudged him. Why was he reminding her they were there? She'd kick them out faster than you could say, 'swift kick in the pants'.

"Oh, they don't know what hard work is," she said, with a flap of the hand, as if that conversation was dead as a doornail. "So unless you own a talent agency and they'll work for free?"

"No, we don't. But we were wondering if you might need a Rosalind and Orlando? We can offer our services," Clark said.

"Humbly," Esther added. She made an awkward half bow.

Bettina stopped, and looked back and forth between them. "Do I know you?" she asked Esther.

"I was in here the other day, um, cleaning windows."

"Not a journalist, are you?"

"No, I'm not. I'm an... actress." It trailed off at the end and she had to admit it didn't sound very convincing.

Bettina looked them both over and wrinkled her nose as if she had to step over a large turd on the footpath. "Well, I guess beggars can't possibly be choosers," she said. "Give me ten minutes, and meet me out the back."

They stood at the side of the hall.

"She's probably having a ciggie," a kind-looking man said, over his shoulder. He was looking at a menu on his laptop.

"Yeah, she likes to pretend she isn't, but you can't hide the smell forever," the woman with reddish hair put in.

"She's drinking again, too. We all get to know each other quite well, don't we, Poppy?"

Esther and Clark exchanged a look. That was what they were counting on.

Over the other side of the room, a bright purple cast caught her eye. The person sporting it had her face hidden by a dark red book. When Esther got closer, she recognised Cara from the local library. She was also a witch in the Ledstow coven. Cara placed the book on her lap, stopping to insert an exquisite bookmark, before closing it with care.

"You were the one who broke their ankle!" Esther exclaimed.

"Yes. It's fractured in three places." Cara tucked her

brown hair behind her ear. She sounded quite proud of the fact.

Esther made sympathetic noises.

"I'm quite fine. I've never broken anything before in my life. People offer to bring you snacks," she whispered. "Which I could definitely get used to. You're one of my lovely library patrons, aren't you?"

"Yes, I am." Esther nodded. She thought it was a little strange that Cara didn't remember exactly who she was, but didn't mind too much, considering that Esther had checked out 'Murder Investigation for Dumbos' the last time they saw each other. "Lottie told me that one of the leading actors had broken their ankle. Wait, how did it happen?"

"Yes, this was my chance to have a really meaty role and I was going to be acting opposite Harding Castle! Poor Harding," she added as it seemed to hit her again that he was gone. She sighed. "Well, I was running through a scene with him and it was pretty late at night. He was a really thorough actor. He leapt forward, getting into his role, and I fell off the stage. Not his fault. He felt absolutely awful. It was my fault really, for standing with my back to where the audience would be. That's a big no-no."

"But what caused it? Did he get scared by something?"

"Harding? Scared? Did you meet the guy?"

She gave a half laugh, remembering that she'd said she

knew him. "Anyway, we're about to audition for the roles. So we'll see you on the other side."

She made a sound of disbelief. "Good luck to you! Bettina's in one of her moods today, so try not to take it personally."

Esther took a deep breath. That sounded bad, but she had a little something witchy up her sleeve.

"Down the end, please," Bettina said, gesturing down a hallway at the back with dressing rooms on either side. It opened up into a plain room with wooden chairs around the sides.

Bettina passed them a script each. "We'll do the scene where they're discussing time. Here. Then we'll get straight into the first song halfway down the page." She made her way to a row of chairs without so much as a 'stand here' or any explanation about the characters.

Esther brushed a stray hair out of her face. "First, I'd like to say that I'm a massive fan of the play. And Clark here has a fantastic memory. It would mean a great deal to us if you'd consider us."

Bettina took her seat and waved her hand to get them to hurry up.

Esther quickly scanned the script. She knew the scene in the original play, Shakespeare's *As You Like It*. Rosalind, fearing danger in the forest, was pretending to be Ganymede. She'd seen poetry about herself nailed to the trees by a lovesick Orlando.

It looked as if this version had Rosalind pretending to be a drunk young person, sitting hunched over in a chair, at a music festival, while Orlando was a singer, looking over his songs before he performed. All of the songs were about Rosalind. It was a complex scene to start with. She needed a few moments to read it all over.

Clark looked down at the script and over to her, with a barely perceptible shrug.

"When you're ready," came Bettina's voice from the seats.

An old man sat down at the piano, his head hunched forward so that it was almost touching the songbook. At Bettina's word, he put his hands over the keys, and started playing. He wasn't looking at the music in front of him or the keys and Esther found it fascinating to watch, so that she missed her starting note by just a beat.

Clark read out his line in the wrong tone of voice and Esther cringed. She thought it was an alright performance, but not wonderful.

Bettina shuffled her script notes and her gaze floated off to the right. This was bad.

They started the song, which was to the tune of Row

Your Boat. It was easy enough to sing and would give Bettina an idea of their voices. At the end of the song, Esther nodded at Clark.

"That's what we're here for," he sang, as they had practised. At home last night, she had drawn a picture of them acting together. That made it easier to get the details right. She only hoped it would work. She visualised Clark and her on stage together in their costumes. The end game. The intention.

"Thank you for listening," she sang, making sure to hit the exact right notes.

It was a little musical magic to help them along, but she had told Clark that this final song was because she wanted to leave an impression.

"By being the weirdest people ever to audition?" he had asked.

"Look, performing is all about being weird. Owning it. Just trust me, please."

He had finally agreed.

"Alright, enough now. What is this extra singing?" Bettina asked, waving her arm through in the air in a gesture to get off the stage. "I'm not entirely convinced that you two have the skills."

Esther sung her piece. "Thank you for your time," making sure that the notes were finished and perfect pitch.

"I said stop."

Esther panicked. The spell wasn't working, either. Why had she thought she could do magic when she needed to? She wasn't a real witch, after all.

"Come over here," Bettina called. Looking down at her notes, she breathed out, in a long-suffering sigh. Then took another huge breath. "But I suppose 'there's small choice in rotten apples,'" she grumbled.

Esther blinked.

Clark did a double take as if he'd heard wrong. "What?"

"It means let's give it a try. On a probationary basis."

"Thank you. And thank you again." Esther pumped her fist, excited that she was going to be in a production with all the excitement that went with that, as well as being able to find out more about what had happened with Harding. "We won't let you down."

"Keep those scripts and start learning them tonight, if you can. We'll be straight into practising tomorrow. You two have a lot of work to do to keep up with the rest." She strode off.

"I didn't think we did that well," Clark said, out of the corner of his mouth.

Esther didn't think so, either. And she couldn't possibly be sure whether Bettina had just changed her mind or whether it was the spell.

The old man at the piano stood up after Bettina had left the room. Esther looked over at the fine silver hair and rumpled shirt. She hadn't seen him without his wife before, so it took a few moments for her to place him. Moran. The man from the quilting club and the interfering Ledstow coven.

"Interesting," he said, simply, with a slight crease of his eyes, and turned to walk slowly from the room.

Esther clapped her hand to her mouth. Moran was magical, but whether he was witch, wizard, mage or sorcerer she didn't know. He had seen her attempt to use her magic to influence Bettina. That wasn't ideal.

"How did you go?" Cara asked them, when she spotted them on the way out. She looked ready to offer them sympathy.

"We got it," Esther said, enjoying the look of surprise that passed over Cara's features.

"Really?"

"I'm as surprised as you," Clark said.

"Don't be so modest," Esther said.

"Great. You two have met Cara," Bettina said from behind her. "She can help you with your lines since we don't have much time. Can't you, Cara?"

"That's absolutely fine. The least I can do. You're very brave taking on the role so close to showtime." There was the slightest hint of a question in the statement.

"I could see that you all needed help. And the play is for charity."

"Well, thank you both. You'll love the play. It's all

adapted for the 21st century and all the songs were written by our very own Moran."

Esther smiled, but she couldn't help wondering whether the line between brave and stupid was sometimes a little smudged.

When she got outside, Clark was already at the corner of the road. He waited there for her, presumably because he wanted it to look like they weren't in cahoots.

"Somehow, we did it," he said, when she reached him.

"We did." A warm feeling of achievement spread through her, but it wasn't matched in the set of Clark's grim expression.

"Now, we just have to pull this off."

"Yup," she said, grinning.

"Why do I get the feeling that you're enjoying this a little too much?" Clark asked her. "Oh, hey, Mick."

This last comment was to a huge man who reached out to shake Clark's hand as he went past.

"Almost didn't realise it was you, without your cop clothes."

"What are you up to, mate?"

The man rubbed his fingers together to make the sign for money. "Same old, same old. I'm off to see about some runners at The Gatehouse."

"Good luck, then. How are your wee critters?"

"They're making me dress up as Maui for their *Moana* birthday party." He chuckled. "See you, boss."

"Who was that?" Esther asked.

"Mick. He does a bit of collections work. Handy lad to know, but he's a big teddy bear. Just don't tell the people he's trying to get money from."

♫

"You're what?" Aria lifted her perfectly threaded eyebrows and stretched her arms out along the back of the couch. Esther had just made them both a strong cup of black tea.

She was waiting for the usual laugh, but her friend didn't sound amused.

"I have to help," Esther said, by way of explanation.

Aria had Louis curled into a vibrating fluffy ball on her lap. "So you're really involved in another murder case? You don't have to do this just to impress Clark, you know. We all know you crave approval." She took a sip of her tea and put the cup back down, sweet as pie.

"Rude," Esther said. "Do you think so little of me?"

"There you go again." Her friend elbowed her and a couple of drops sloshed over the edge of her cup.

"Aria!"

"Oops, sorry. Look, you know I love you, sweetie, I just don't want you to put yourself in any danger."

Esther grabbed a cloth from the kitchen and dabbed at the spots. "I don't think I'm doing anything that risky.

I'm going to be acting in a play, that's all. Spouting some lines. Singing some songs."

"Hanging around on a daily basis with a maniac who killed someone, potentially. Learning lines with a murderer. Singing with a slayer. Dancing with a destroyer." She huffed out a breath of air. "Alright. It's just that I'm going through some stuff myself right now. I don't have the mental space to cope with your problems too."

"Oh, I didn't realize," Esther said, a wave of guilt crashing over her. She had been a little preoccupied with their plan for the play. "I'm sorry. We didn't even get to your intentions for the year."

"My only goal is to get through this wedding without any deaths or dismemberments. I've got six months."

"Easy," Esther said.

Aria shook her head. "You're underestimating my family's knack for drama. Remember my 21st birthday when my cousin wrote the wrong date on the invitation so half of the family didn't turn up?"

Esther suppressed a laugh.

"And don't even mention the engagement party."

An uncomfortable twinge of guilt made Esther shrug her shoulders, thinking of the party where people had started spouting their biggest secrets. She had found out later that it was her fault, since she had accidentally played a musical spell for honesty. She decided to confess now, while her friend had a mouthful of sweet treats. It would give her at least a few seconds' reprieve.

"That might have been my fault," she began. "When I was playing music, I cast a spell to get people to tell the truth. I only wanted to figure out who killed Rochelle. I should have told you earlier."

Aria took a long sip of tea, swallowed, and asked, "You did that?"

Esther nodded. "It was an accident."

"You made those people say things they'd kept secret for so long! I'm so proud of you. That is really impressive." She waved away Esther's apologies. "Yes, it did cause me some heartache at the time and Troy is still sulking a little, but it's better to have it all out in the open now, rather than later."

"Thank you for being so good about this. I've felt so terrible," Esther said, reaching out to place her hand on her friend's. "And yes, I think it is better to have everything on the table before you're married. Now I just need to figure out how to cast spells when I want to, instead of at the worst possible time. Shall we meet up tomorrow?"

Aria stroked Louis, and he rolled onto his back, like an innocent baby. She even tickled his tummy. No one else was allowed to do that. "Yeah, sure, I'll meet you at the local after work?"

"I'll ask Ash too."

"Perfect."

"Right. I better read over these lines a hundred times," she said, gesturing at her script, which was lying on the table.

"Good luck, love."

"I hopefully have a few days to learn it," Esther said. "I can do this."

*L*ater that night, Bettina messaged them all saying that there were two new actors and that there was going to be an emergency rehearsal in the morning.

"It's not much notice. What would happen if we had plans?" She had asked Clark on the phone, after the actors' group chat came up and started pinging with messages. "I don't know if I can do this."

"No, it's not. But I think the play comes first from now on. We have to treat it like it's as important to us as our jobs. It's only fair on all the others who are giving up their time."

"You're right," Esther said, trying not to question what they had gotten themselves into. It was all her idea, after all, and it would all be over in a few weeks. Hopefully, a killer would be caught and they would all be a little safer.

"Have you read over the script? I think I've got the first half memorised."

"Already? Yeah, I've read it. I absolutely adore the script." The play was modernised, and it also played up the relationship between Rosalind and Celia. It was less about gender-swapping and more about love in all its forms. "And we also have to send profile photos to Lee's email address. I wonder what for?"

"It's probably for promo. It could be helpful for us in identifying the suspects. I've definitely ruled out the wife. I looked into her quite heavily, because a crime like this is often done by the spouse. Wendy seems like a really practical person. She wouldn't hurt a fly and she talked about Harding all the time. She was well off on her own merits, so she didn't need to stay with him financially. Sometimes it can be for the life insurance, you see. Several people have confirmed that he's not the type of person to have a mistress, so I don't think it's revenge."

Esther was impressed. "Great. But how do they know for sure if he's the type of person?"

"Well, it just means it's not the first avenue we check. We can now look at friends and colleagues, because we know that the door being locked meant that Harding had let someone in. So it had to be someone he knew well."

"Yes, the timing suggests that it is someone in the play.

It happened just before the first big rehearsal. And he was due to be visited by two of the production members."

"Or it could be a workmate," he said, not quite convinced. "I finally got in touch with the Head of Parapsyc at the university. It's exactly as I thought. Edwards wants me to give him a full research proposal by the end of the month."

"Oh, what are you going to do?"

"Well, I'd really like to study precognition. That's fascinating stuff."

"Have you heard back from the mystery email sender?"

"Not yet." He let out a sigh. "Edwards is paying my wages for this year, so I need to give him something. He won't be very keen for me to stay here if he doesn't see some tangible research."

As Esther walked up Grange Way the next morning, she thought about Harding. His killer had to be someone associated with the play. She just had to get to know everyone well enough in the limited time she had, that they'd somehow confess to her.

Fog clung to the fields and trees, turning the greens and browns of Ledstow to a whitewashed grey. She rubbed her hands together to warm them.

The hall was freezing cold as ancient halogen heaters reluctantly turned on with a ticking noise. No one seemed to notice Esther, so she introduced herself. Lee smiled briefly at her. Cara eyed her over the top of her book.

Poppy, the young woman with the strawberry blonde hair, came in and slumped dramatically onto the couch. "My life is over."

Esther kept her voice upbeat. "What's up?"

"Oh, hello new person," she said. "Just… have you ever been on a date and everything went perfectly and then they just don't call?"

"No," Cara said, putting her book down. "I have an excellent feeling for these things. If we're not into it, I don't even stay. I would say something like, 'Sorry, it seems like this isn't going to work out. I'd rather not waste both of our time.'"

Poppy laughed. "I love that. And does it work?"

"It does, actually. I think we've been conditioned to be nice, but people actually appreciate the directness. Except for one guy, a butcher, who tried to convince me that it was going to work between us. But he wasn't impressed when I said I was a vegetarian."

"I thought you were taken now, anyway?" Poppy asked.

"Oh, I am. Taken," she said, with a secret smile.

"When are we going to meet him?"

"Probably on opening night. He said he wanted to come."

"She has been telling us how hot he is the entire time," Poppy added. "She won't shut up about it."

Esther wanted to keep it on track. "I'd love to hear more about everyone here. Who is flirting with whom? Who should we avoid?"

"Well, I'd keep away from Bettina if you can. She is a real—" Poppy said.

"I've met her a couple of times, already." Esther took a mental note that there was no love lost there. "She seems really determined."

"You can't really avoid her. She is the hammer that shapes reality, to badly paraphrase Brecht," Cara said.

"I don't even know what that means, Cara." Poppy counted the actors off on her fingers. "But, basically, Lee is the favourite. Scottie is that really built guy over there."

She pointed to a man with spiky light, brown hair who looked to be in his forties. She thought it was the one who had been looking at a menu the last time.

"And we've got young Roman with the blond hair, who likes Poppy," Cara put in. "Can't forget him." Esther filed that away.

"Don't say it," Poppy said, affectionately. "It doesn't help that he plays my love interest, as well. Why can't it be the ones I like who are hanging on my every word?"

"Do you think maybe you go for the bad boys?" Cara

asked, but she said it quietly as the man she'd pointed at was walking towards them.

Roman was the very dictionary definition of clean cut. His hair was swept to the side as if he had just stepped out of a salon and his clothes seemed like they were bought that very day. Esther couldn't help but glance down at her own jeans and top which were slightly crumpled and had some sauce splotches on them.

"Who's that?" Poppy asked, as Clark came in and shook hands with Bettina and Scottie. Esther tried to catch his eye, but he was doing a good job of pretending he didn't know her.

She shrugged.

"Right, thespians," Bettina said, and everyone moved stealthily to where they should be, gradually blending into the background. Esther didn't know where she should be, so she moved back towards the wall until her backside hit into the wood panel.

Bettina issued commands for the next five minutes and everyone scattered to follow them. "Poppy, why haven't you got your prop? Moran, did you get a replacement tree for the set? I want today to be absolutely spot on. Right, from the top."

When it came to her turn, Esther stood frozen to the spot, as she tried to recall a single line.

Bettina pointed a finger at her. "You can do it with the script today," she said, marching over and thrusting some paper at her. "But we'll be wanting to see you knowing the lines by the end of the weekend."

"I can help you. Maybe tomorrow?" Cara whispered to her.

"Thanks," she said. "I need it."

"Finish this one off. Then run through again. And make everything bigger, people. Bigger. Larger." She circled her arms in an expansive motion. "I have to see it from the back row. My grandmother's grandmother needs to see it from the back row without her spectacles."

After the final song, there was a part where Poppy had to do a monologue. Everyone else waited around the edges, sitting or standing, while she finished off her lines.

Cara was sitting at the edge of the room. "You need to speak up a bit louder," Cara said to her, patting her stomach. "Really project your voice. Make it come from down here." She lowered her voice to a baritone.

"Thanks. I am trying," Esther said.

"You've got a gorgeous singing voice. But do you have much acting experience?" She turned to regard Esther with shrewd eyes.

"Not really," she admitted.

"Why did you want to do the play so badly, then?" Cara asked, but it was casual in tone, not suspicious.

Esther shrugged. "No time like the present. I'd always wanted to do one."

After they'd been practising for what felt like a long

time, Lee walked past, holding a large sandwich, which he gave to Bettina. Poppy was just leaving the stage and she stared after him.

"Hungry?" Esther asked.

"Yeah, I guess I am. That's just mean."

"Hopefully, we can finish soon."

It was two o'clock when they finally finished, and only because Bettina was called away by a woman with a dress over her arm, who was presumably the Head of Costuming.

"Are we calling it a day, Mrs V?" Moran asked, from his spot at the piano.

"Oh, fine. Next one is tomorrow at 1pm. Don't be late, for the sake of the theatre gods!" She disappeared around the corner and they all breathed a sigh of relief.

Esther paused to have a drink and then leant down to put her drink bottle in her bag. A hand brushed lightly over the back of her hair and she saw Clark walk out the door. She caught up outside but he didn't slow his pace at all.

"Hey," she puffed.

"Do I know you?" he asked. "Oh, you're from the play?"

She laughed. "We only need to act like we're acquaintances. Not that we don't know each other at all. It's a little town. Everyone knows everyone, anyway."

"It's safer to pretend we're only just meeting. We don't want people to start putting two and two together."

Esther let out a breath. He really was frustrating. "How do you think the run-through went today?"

"It wasn't great. But I talked to Scottie and a few of the chorus line. They seemed to think Harding was one of those types who name-drop celebrities all the time."

"Well, I didn't find out anything much so far. But I think it's going to be a good way to find out what really went on. We just need to stick it out."

CHAPTER 7

On the morning of the second rehearsal, Esther's phone rang. She was feeding Jay, tapping seeds into the lid she used for his bowl. She added a peanut in its shell as a treat. Apparently, blue jays also liked mealworms, but she refused to keep those in her house.

"Gourmet seeds for you, sir," she said out loud. "Again."

Her phone played *Ride of the Valkyries* from the bench and Jay fluffed his feathers up in fright.

"Good morning," she said.

"I'm not going to make it to the rehearsal today," Clark said. "Please send my apologies."

"To Bettina? Do you ever want to see me alive again?"

"Yes, of course I'd like to see you alive. And very much

nak—" He broke off. "Uh, yes, Shona. Five minutes. Thank you."

Esther suppressed a laugh. She heard a door close on the other end of the phone.

"Ahem, sorry about that." He lowered his voice. "I know that I'm not going to be popular but I've got some leads to follow up pretty quickly. I'll let you know what has happened with the case. You recall that you asked about Harding's wife early on? Well, she was the one who called in the body. But that was the day after he died." He paused. "Remember I got the call after we went out for lunch on that Sunday? So why didn't she notice her husband never came to bed? Why didn't she notice he was flat on his back in her kitchen until midday the next day?"

Esther sucked in her breath. "I don't know. It doesn't sound great for her."

"She originally stated that she had gone to sleep early and woken up late, which was feasible, if not probable. She said she had fallen asleep in the lounge after a few wines."

And slept through until lunch? Without hearing anything at all? Esther thought that was a stretch.

"But she came into the station today and told us that she wanted to tell the truth. Get this. She was not, in fact, in the house. She was fighting with her husband and had stayed at her sister's place that night. Her sister has backed this up, too."

Esther sucked in her breath. "Oh dear," she managed. It was using all her strength not to brag that she was right about the pyjamas.

"You can see why she didn't want to own up to it. I'll be pushing to turn this into a murder investigation now that we have a prime suspect and some sort of motive."

"What were they fighting about?" She turned away and leaned back against the kitchen bench.

"That's what we're trying to establish. Hopefully, she'll play ball since she came to us in the first place. It's a strange business, because I think the time of death might have been around when we heard that scream."

Esther felt more than a little sympathy for the wife. If she was innocent, it would be nerve-wracking being questioned by Shona and Clark. She had been there, done that, and had the badge to prove it.

"Well, good luck." Esther's own listening approach seemed to work just fine. People told her things. "Sing out if you need me to work my, ah, magic."

"I will not," he said. "You have a good day."

Esther pressed the 'End Call' button. Perhaps he didn't like the idea that she would be better at pulling secrets from a suspect than him.

"Work my magic," chirped a voice from near the floor

that sounded very much like Jay. Esther turned around. The bird couldn't talk, could it?

Nope. She shook her head. She didn't have time for that sort of nonsense.

♫

THE SECOND REHEARSAL was marginally better than the first. Esther managed to remember some of her lines and even got some praise out of Bettina.

"That will do," Bettina said, looking directly at Esther.

"Did you see that? That means you did great," Cara said, when Esther came over to her spot by the wall. "She even nodded at you. You'll be the new favourite soon, I swear." She reached a finger into the top of her cast to itch the skin. "Stupid thing. I can't wait until it's off."

Scottie came over after he finished his part. "I've got to go early today. Who'd like to remind Bettina for me?"

"Oh yeah, today's the big day. That one's up to you. He's opening a restaurant," she explained to Esther.

"Here in town?"

"Yeah. I'm giving it a go, anyway. It might flop completely." Scottie shrugged.

"That's so cool, though. An exciting step."

"I'd never worked in a restaurant before, but always loved to cook. It was actually Harding who offered to become my partner and put in some cash. He came over for dinner with his wife and they raved about my cooking. He convinced me to take the plunge."

"You'll be great, Scottie," Cara said.

"Congratulations," said a voice. It was the woman with the dyed red hair.

"Cheers."

"Helen, have you met Esther yet? She's playing Rosalind."

The woman turned to Esther. "No, I haven't. Nice to meet you," she said. "I'll meet with you soon to talk about your hair." With that, she left.

Esther thought it was interesting that Scottie's restaurant was funded by Harding. It seemed like a sort of generosity that was at odds with the impression that Esther had of Mr. Castle so far.

ESTHER WAS STILL THINKING about it as she approached the bar at their local pub, the Twig and Berries, after rehearsal. The bartender raised his brows in greeting. She reddened, remembering that last time when he had caught her eavesdropping. But he'd never mentioned it.

"I see you're getting involved in the theatre world now," he said, picking up one of the flyers from a pile on the bar and handing it to her, with a grin. Her own face was staring back at her from the ad. 'As You Like It - New and Improved' read the headline. That was fast work by Lee to get the promotional fliers out.

"Yes, I am," she said. "I've just come from rehearsal, actually."

He flipped a glass the right way up with a practised hand. "Talented lady. I think, today, you might need an overloaded bowl of chips. And a pint of lager. How does that sound?"

"Um, yeah. And two more pints for my friends, thanks." By now, she was used to the bartender knowing what she wanted. It seemed to be his badge of honour, and it was useful if she was feeling indecisive, which happened more often than not.

He put his hand out. "I'm Jeremiah. What's your name?"

"Esther."

"I've heard you sing karaoke. You're not bad."

"Thanks," she said, finding it funny that 'not bad' meant high praise for most.

"We'll bring them over," he said, after she had paid.

She walked past the fireplace, pausing for a second to warm up, before heading over to her friends.

Aria was sitting with Ashton in their usual table in the back corner. Esther placed the glasses carefully in a clump in the middle of the table, and moved the dirty glasses onto another table to be picked up. Ashton looked up when she came over.

"Have you booked any more gigs for us?"

"I just bought your round of drinks," she said. "No, I haven't. I'm sure we can play at my nan's rest home any time. But I'm going in a slightly different direction right at the moment." She held up the flier. "I'm sure you'll both approve of this. But after that is all done, yes. We can play all the gigs."

Ashton peered at the image. "That's you. What the—" He grabbed for the flier but she held it out of his reach, then folded it up and put it in her coat pocket.

"It's quite a long story."

"I have so many questions, Essie."

"That's not all. She's getting involved in a murder case again," Aria put in. "Can you believe it? I think it's some sort of subconscious need for approval to impress her mum, Her Honour the Judge. Getting into the justice system like your mummy? Or is it to impress that cop?"

"Chips and gravy. My first loves," Ash said, when Jeremiah put the bowl down on the table.

Esther elbowed her friend just as she was about to drink her drink and some slopped onto the table. Aria froze and looked up at her. They both burst out laughing and couldn't stop for a few minutes.

"Beer is... coming out my nose." Esther said.

Ashton grabbed some serviettes and wiped up the table and passed one to each of them with a long-suffering sigh.

When they had somewhat recovered their dignity, Esther turned to Aria. "So, love, tell us what's happening with you? We came here to talk about you, not me. I see Troy has been posting about how lucky he is to have you on his social media."

Aria heaved a sigh. She grabbed her handbag and started riffling through, until she found her lip gloss. She began applying the cherry colour between sentences, which Esther knew meant she was upset.

"Being engaged is really hard. Like, I know the wedding is not for a few months.... But we are both trying to plan things.... and to be honest, we are taking different tasks. And just doing them...."

"Well, that sounds good, at least." Esther grabbed a chip and bit into the salty hot snack.

"No, it's like we both don't really give a damn about the wedding... I was in charge of the invitations and I just chose a lime green and silver without agonising over it. Troy was meant to be choosing the desserts and he did it without a second thought. And we're both working a lot to pay for this wedding. We hardly even see each other. It's not even going to be that big, only about 250 people. And that's mostly just my family." Esther knew she wasn't exaggerating. "Some of my aunties were upset they weren't invited to the engagement party so we have had to invite them. They gossiped to my grandma about it."

"It sounds like you need to chat to each other."

"Shouldn't we care a little more about these choices? I just keep thinking that if we can't plan this together, how are we going to do anything that a married couple does together?"

"You two have lived together for ages," Esther said gently. "You've probably already done lots of those things successfully."

"My sister said that planning a wedding was the most stressful thing she ever did. And she's got triplets," Ashton said. "That's part of the reason why Will and I will probably nip off to a tropical island."

"Also — and this is going to sound whack-a-doodle — the universe is giving me signs that I should be with other people."

"Other people? Like who?" Ashton said.

"Do not listen to the universe this time," Esther said.

Aria heaved a sigh. "Anyway, that's enough about me. Onto more exciting topics. Have you slept with the cop yet?" she asked, brightening as she turned the attention back away from herself.

"It's complicated."

"That means you have," said Ashton.

She shook her head. "It was all on at the end of last year, and we've been chatting to each other every day. But he was a bit funny the other day at lunch. He wasn't exactly distant but almost, like, just at the edge of the friend zone. Hot and cold."

"Lunch? Do you expect him to be all over you while eating club sandwiches?"

"Not all over me, no," she replied, giving Ashton a look.

"Did he spend New Year's Eve with someone else?" Aria said, sympathetically.

"No, he stayed home."

"That's what he said." Aria pursed her lips.

Esther shook her head. "He looks after his younger sister, Triss. He's her guardian."

"What happened to their parents?"

"Well, I'm not sure, exactly. I know his mum passed away. I think his dad is still around. We mostly just talk about the case, to be honest. And now, the play. Which is part of the case."

"Have you actually communicated that you want more, Essie?" Ashton asked, rolling his eyes.

Esther considered this. She had been saying she wasn't going to date anyone and she was perfectly happy with her single status. Until she had fallen for the policeman investigating the case and it was suddenly 'all on'. Clark had certainly seemed pretty interested at Christmastime. Then there was the drunken 'almost kiss'.

Did she want a relationship? She definitely wanted something.

Her friends always told her she needed to be more

direct. But how could she be clear about what she wanted if she didn't know herself?

♫

LATER THAT NIGHT, her phone vibrated on the nightstand when Esther had just picked up her book. She put it down on the bed and looked over at the screen. It was Clark.

"Burning the midnight oil?" she asked.

"It's only… nine o'clock. I've just left work. I've been doing some background work on the Castles. Cross checking against things that Wendy said, and it seems like she's telling the truth."

"Ooh, what did she say?"

"The fight that they had was about his health. The doctor told him he had to change things. He thought he'd be fine keeping on exactly as he was. His wife said that she'd been on at him for a long time to start eating better and doing some exercise. This had been going on for four years. He still thought he was in his prime."

"Oh, right."

Louis didn't seem to like that she'd changed position, so he walked gingerly up her legs and stood on her lap, with his tail up. She stroked the silver back.

"Unfortunately, that fits with the medical causes theory. So it doesn't help our case."

"That's true," she said thoughtfully.

"She said something else, which may be relevant. She said she would ask him who he really was when nobody else was watching. He thought that was silly. But she wanted him to tell her anything about himself. She wouldn't have minded if he said that he wanted to open a carrot-flavoured cupcake shop, as long as it was true."

"Okay," she said. "Poor lady."

"Oh, Wendy can look after herself, I think. Also… I wanted to chat to you about something, Esther."

That sounded very formal. The pause seemed to drag as she wondered what it could be.

"I know that we've been getting to know each other for a short time, and it's not the usual way of things. Would you like to come over for dinner and meet Triss? She's quite bubbly and loud, but—"

"Yes. I'd love to." She was so surprised at the question that she burst out with it.

Louis finally settled into a ball and began vibrating with a low purr.

"Good. Does this weekend work? Sunday night? I'll make it at seven so we have a bit of time after the practice."

"The show is coming up fast."

"My dad will be there, too. He usually comes over on a Sunday."

Not only was she going to meet Clark's sister. She was

going to meet his dad. She didn't really know anything about them.

Before then, there was a lot of work to do. She had to do a shift at the music shop and the next week promised a gruelling schedule of play rehearsals.

"Mick came into work again today, to tell me about some stolen vehicles. He went to The Gatehouse and the lad that left his bill unpaid was a Chase Russell. He was also suspected of doing some vandalism a week or so ago. Then he just disappeared, leaving a big fat bill behind him."

"Alright," Esther said, slowly.

"I'm going in there tomorrow to find out more."

"Can I join you?"

"I wouldn't expect any less," he said, with a sigh.

"Good night."

CHAPTER 8

The music shop was quiet. Esther had already counted the drumsticks and the reeds. Twice. She had unpacked all of the extra stock of music books in the storeroom and tucked the new ones into the shelves. She had tidied up the trumpets and discussed guitar solos with Mark from the cheese shop. It was a pretty standard shift.

When he left, she rung up her grandmother.

"Hello, darling."

"Nan, I'm going to be one of the starring roles in the local production."

"Are you really? What is it?"

"*As You Like It*. But it's an abridged and modernised musical. Short and sweet. As you like it and have never seen it before!"

"Clever girl. Can I come and watch the play?"

"Of course. But you'll have to make your own way there. I'll be busy before and after. Will that be alright?"

"Fine, fine. I can ask the nurse here. When I said you were a musical witch, I didn't think you'd take it quite so literally," her nan said, her voice filled with amusement.

"Good one, nan."

"You'll catch up to me one day, Blue Eyes."

Esther laughed. "Cheeky."

"Hey, I read on the community page that people have seen eyes glowing in the darkness. A few people in upper Ledstow reported it."

"That's a new one. Is everybody ripping into them in the replies?"

"Well, yes. They are. But be sure to be careful, alright?"

"Alright, nan."

She was just thinking about shutting the shop for an early lunch break when the front door bell dinged.

It was her best friend, Ashton. He plonked a box on the counter and the fragrant smell of korma curry rose up around her.

"Oh, you're a godsend, Ash. What spice level is it?"

"I got medium for you," he said. "And I've got a gig organised for us on Saturday the 18th. Get your ukelele ready," Ashton said, waggling his eyebrows at her.

"But that's the closing night of the play," Esther said.

"What's the gig?" She picked up the curry box and took it out the back, then rustled through the drawer for two forks. She scooped half of the curry and rice onto a plate and gave the box to Ash.

"Oh, I forgot." He sat down at the table. "It was just a 40th birthday party. Do you remember Steph from the salon? It's not paid or anything. But if you can't, that's not a problem. I'll tell her we are not available. Steph will have to put up with inferior entertainment." He took a huge forkful of rice.

Esther considered for a moment. "You can still do it! And if you talk nicely to them, you might be able to make it late enough that I could come after the performance for a finale."

He chewed his mouthful. "No, don't worry about it. You'll have the wrap party, won't you?"

"I suppose I will," she said. "You do it, though. Please."

"Next time," he said. "I wouldn't go and perform without you. Soulful is both of us, or not at all."

Ashton smiled at her. He wasn't making her feel guilty at all, but a little twinge behind her neck said she should take these opportunities while she had them.

Sometimes, she felt like she was spread so thin that she wasn't doing well in any of the areas of her life.

Work was fine. Her boss trusted her to run the shop and do some of the management tasks but it also felt like he didn't respect her very much. She could admit that her love life was blossoming, if she didn't muck it up. Her family was, well, her family.

Solving mysteries got her heart rate pumping. It was fascinating finding out what secrets people hid. She still didn't know what it was about her that made people talk to her, but something did.

And music was her lifeblood. Without music, who was she?

"After this play is done, I promise we are going to focus on our music careers. I'll find us some gigs, and we'll rock them."

"Of course we will," Ashton said, comfortably. Nothing seemed to faze him.

♫

SHE MET Clark outside the police station after her shift. He had a black folder under his arm. He smiled when he saw her.

"It's just around here," he said. "In the old city walls."

They walked around the corner and stopped outside the whitestone gate house. "Maybe let me handle this one," he said.

"I didn't hear you," she said, walking ahead through the archway and turning left at a black doorway with a sign over it. She pulled the door open.

"Hello, darling. Do you two need a room?" The person

behind the counter was sitting in a wheelchair. Her long, grey hair flowed down over the shoulders of her denim jacket. She was wearing a Metallica tee shirt underneath and she had a tattoo on her wrist, which revealed itself when she flipped open the room register. Esther immediately liked her.

"Hi, Dot," Clark said.

The woman lifted her glasses up to look at who was talking. "The young policeman!"

"I stayed here when I first moved to town six months ago," Clark said to Esther. "Dot was really kind."

"He helped me more than I helped him," she said, smiling, so that her eyes crinkled at the edges.

"I ended up being a pallbearer when her husband died, too."

"And you carried all his old shed stuff out so we could sell it."

"Dot, we are actually looking for someone who might be staying here. My mate Mick mentioned you might know something." He leaned over the counter to sneak a look at the register.

She snatched it close to her chest. "Nope, nothing."

"Come on, Dot."

The woman looked down and very carefully shut the register book. "Well, you know I can't give you that information," she said, lining the pen up carefully. "But I take the register with me on my lunch break, so I know which rooms need cleaning. And I sit out in the wee courtyard and eat my lunch for half an hour at noon each day. Sometimes I'm so forgetful that I leave it out there. Anyway, that's enough about me. What about you?"

"I'm doing fine," he said, pleasantly. "I'll come chat to you one day when you're in a better mood."

"You do that."

When they got outside, he said, "It's a pity she never gives me any information. I just hope she hasn't changed the spot where she hides the gate key."

"Really unhelpful," Esther agreed, with a grin. She wondered if Dot was friends with her grandmother. If not, she had to introduce them.

CHAPTER 9

The next morning, Esther got up early to practise her lines. She walked back and forth in the living room, stopping every now and then to eat crackers topped with cheddar. Louis watched her from the couch, a foul look on his face. Jay was on his usual spot at the top of the bookshelves.

"Oh my gosh, I'll never get this," she said to Jay, who was looking at her with his head cocked to the side.

Esther started her line, then stopped and put her hands on her hips.

From behind her, the bird squawked something that sounded a lot like the rest of the line.

"What was that?" she asked, absurdly. "Are you holding out on me?"

There was a knock on the door. Esther shut the bird in the bathroom, with some difficulty.

"Hi Cara," she said, letting her in.

Cara spread her arms out. She was dressed in a beautiful long, black dress, with her purple cast sticking out the bottom. Her dark green coat looked amazing with the green streak at the front of her hair, which was piled up in a knot on her head.

"Wow."

"Who were you talking to?"

"Oh, just practising."

"How are the lines going? You're so good for taking this on with so little notice. We're all so happy the production can still happen. Especially Mrs V!"

"This is really hard," Esther admitted, shrugging slightly. "I don't know what I was thinking. You don't want to pat Louis!" She blurted it out as Cara made an 'aww' sound and advanced towards the silver kitten, then stopped, hands on hips, as she eyed up the little cat, deciding whether it was a threat.

"You're going to be fine," she said to Esther. "Even if you mess up your lines, your singing will be enough to carry the whole thing. A few of us were talking about it after the rehearsal the other day."

Esther smiled. "Thank you. But it won't save me from looking like some sort of fish up there on the stage, opening and closing my mouth. A dancing fish, maybe."

A noise that sounded suspiciously like a bird pecking at a door came from the bathroom.

"You're getting it. You'll be fine," Cara said, looking towards the noise. "What is that?"

"Ah, did you know Harding very well?"

"Not well," she replied. "He was a good actor and really well respected. When you started to talk to him, though, you could tell he was a very stuck up man. But people seemed to never say no to him. It's still really sad for his wife."

"His wife is nice, then?"

"Oh, she's truly lovely. I'm not sure what she saw in him. I mean, he's great to have as an actor friend but I'd say he'd be as stubborn as anything."

"And everyone else in the play got on with him?"

"Yes, he was very easy to act with, because he always got it right the first time. Very dedicated to his craft."

"Okay, well let's go through this scene together. I apparently have to meet with Helen, the hair and makeup lady, later."

"I love Helen. She's awesome. But are you coming to the funeral? Harding's funeral, I mean?"

"Oh, when is it?"

"It's today. I thought you would have known." Cara squinted at her, and Esther remembered again that she had said that she was Harding's friend. "One thirty."

"Oh, yeah." This could be an excellent opportunity to listen to people who had known Harding, she thought.

"You're not really dressed for it, though." She indicated Esther's faded trackpants. "Not being rude."

"I'll get changed. Should we go together?"

"Yeah."

After they had run through a few times, Cara seemed happy.

"I'll just get dressed into something nicer. Do you want something to eat? It's sort of lunchtime," Esther said.

"We could get something on the way."

She went into the bedroom and emerged a few moments later, in black pants and a light pink blouse, along with heels.

Cara was sitting on the couch, with the bird perched on her right hand. She was stroking its back with her other hand.

"I knew that I recognised you from somewhere, Esther. You came to our coven meeting."

Jay cocked his head, looking straight at Esther, and opened his mouth. "Work my magic."

"I'M NOT part of the coven," Esther said, for at least the tenth time. They were on the bus heading to the church.

"And I'm not going to join. For one, I'm terrible at sewing. I can't be part of a quilting club. My friend laughed for five minutes straight when I said I'd been to one."

"Did you know that witches are stronger when they do magic in groups?"

"That… is cool," she said, and meant it. "But I'm really new to all of this. I don't know what I'm doing half the time. I made frogs come up out of the ground in the middle of winter. I can't help but think of those poor froggies!"

"We all made mistakes in our baby witch days. Just have a good think about joining, please. We need more people. Lottie doesn't have enough hours in the day and Iris' spells go wrong twice as often as they go right."

"And two, I'm so busy. I have three jobs and now the play as well. Well, two jobs, I suppose. But I'm looking for another one."

"Are you and Clark together?"

She stared at Cara with her mouth open. "Well, I… You knew?"

"I suspected."

Esther lapsed into quiet, as she pondered who else knew. Perhaps they had been a bit more lax than she thought. They'd hoped to get to know the others in the production. But instead they'd revealed things about themselves.

When they were pulling up to the stop, she stood up. Cara still seemed lost in dreamland, sitting in her seat. Esther kicked her toes into the solid cast as she went to get off the bus and pain throbbed in her toes.

"Oh, I am so sorry. I'm such a klutz."

Cara looked up. "That's okay." She didn't move her foot or grimace. Esther thought it must be one strong cast.

The whole interaction left Esther feeling a little bit off, but she couldn't put her finger on why.

Esther gasped as she got out of the bus. The little church was picture perfect. It was on the lower slopes of the hills and the town spread out below. People picked their way along the cobbled path that led through an archway to an old wooden door. The church was so small and quaint, however, that there was no way all of these people were going to fit inside.

Esther looked at the crowd in dismay. She wouldn't be able to find much out, either, with this many people at the funeral. The mourners were mostly older; sixty and above, she thought. The women were dressed in bright colours, the men in elegant suits.

Esther and Cara watched the service from outside, peering in the double doors. Esther heard a lot about Harding's acting roles and standing ovations, excellent reviews and witty things he'd said in interviews. But there wasn't much about who he was as a person. She rubbed her hands together. They remained chilly, even though the winter sun was shining. Cara was quiet.

Afterwards, they found Bettina, who was holding forth in the middle of a circle of people, a tiny cupcake in her hand.

"Dear, dear Harding," she was saying, waving the cake around. "We had so many wonderful times, him and me. And the last thing we were doing together was a little community production. I don't think it will ever be the same."

Somebody had a crush, Esther thought, and her eyes flicked to Harding's wife, Wendy, who was standing by herself, next to the coffin.

Her phone rang. She wandered further away from the crowd as she answered it, towards a small memorial garden.

"I went to look at Dot's register today," Clark said. "I'll spare you the details."

"I do want all the details, but I'm just at Harding's funeral."

"How did you manage that one?" he asked. "Never mind. Talk later."

She put her phone away, and made a beeline for Wendy Castle.

Wendy, Harding's widow, was a comfortable looking woman, with rosy cheeks, soft grey hair curling around her face and the sleeves of her blouse rolled up above her wrists, like she wasn't afraid of hard work. As Esther watched, Wendy reached out as if to tap the top of the casket, but stopped just before she reached it.

"I knew there'd be a lot of people here," she said, when Esther came to stand beside her. "But this is over the top. Everyone came."

"I'm Esther. I'm in the drama society. I've heard from everyone about how Mr Castle was a great man to act with." And a lot more, she thought, but she didn't need to mention that.

"Acting was more than a job for my husband. It was everything. In the rest of his daily life, he was a man of habit. Got up at seven. Breakfast at eight. The newspaper, a walk around the block. But I think he really escaped from that when he acted. He got to be someone else." Wendy's voice trailed off, as if she was looking far into the past.

"I'm really sorry for your loss," Esther said, wondering if she should leave Wendy to it.

"He didn't need those habits when he acted," she continued.

"I understand," Esther said, thinking of the ways she coped with her anxiety.

Wendy looked towards Bettina as she laughed loudly. "He wasn't comfortable in his own skin, I think. He wasn't the easiest person to live with. But he never cheated. That's one thing he was very principled about."

"How did you two meet, if you don't mind me asking?" Wendy had not spoken during the service, instead sitting quietly in the front row, hands folded in her lap, leaving it to Harding's older brother to run down the list of accomplishments. Bettina had also done a very impassioned speech about how privileged she was to work with him.

"When he first began acting in the theatre, he came to Cornwall for the summer. He was having a bit of a crisis. He stayed on my dad's farm, working out in the fields, and he told me that it was the first time he'd ever really felt like someone in his own right. 'Of course you are. Everybody does their bit. Now be quiet and help me set the table,' I said to him." She laughed. "I always told him what I thought. No one else would."

"That sounds rather sensible," Esther said. It also sounded like Harding was trying on another role that summer. The farmboy.

"Well, you've got to trust yourself or nobody will trust you."

"It was a lovely funeral," Esther said, politely. "He must have touched so many people's lives."

She nodded. "He'd have liked to know that, I think. He cared a lot more than people realized. Even me. It's been nice to meet you, Esther." Wendy turned towards the kitchen, already buttoning her sleeves up to the elbows, ready to dive back into work.

Everybody *was* there, Esther thought. That was a good point. But perhaps it was more important to look at who hadn't turned up to the funeral? Helen, for one. Poppy. Nadine, the costume lady. And Lee.

CHAPTER 10

The funeral left Esther drained but she still had to meet with the hair and makeup lady. The dressing room, where Helen had set up her salon, smelled of mothballs. Classical music drifted to her as Esther poked her head in.

Helen had her mouth open and was looking in the mirror.

"Are you ready for me?"

She startled when Esther spoke, but quickly composed herself, patting at her hair.

"Yes, I am, love. Sit," she said, pointing to a chair in front of a mirror. "I've got a sore throat that I just can't shake. I hope you don't mind the music. It helps me work."

"Not at all. Chopin, isn't it? One of the Nocturnes."

"Very good." Helen nodded approvingly.

"I studied music."

"Well, I just like it. Now, your hair," Helen said, staring at her from uncomfortably close, and screwing up her face. "What are we going to do with it?"

Her voice was hoarse and gravelly, as if she used to be a smoker. Helen's top was a mix of loud fabrics in red, black and white, stitched together in a stylish way. The fabric that was a few inches from Esther's face had tiny black question marks marching along a white background.

Esther opened her mouth but apparently it needed no response, because Helen began lifting up locks of her hair and inspecting it. She knew that her hair was lank but that was pretty unnecessary. Esther hoped she didn't have split ends. Helen's own hair was impossibly smooth and that very bright dyed shade of red. She had a long, heart-shaped face.

Helen rubbed the hair between her hands with some sort of pomade, which smelt of chocolate. "So what do you do for a job?"

Esther squirmed. "I work in the music shop here. It's only a stopgap, really."

"Most jobs are," Helen said, with a sigh. "What's the dream then?"

"I'm in a band. It would be nice to record an album, maybe. Play a few more gigs."

She paused to wipe her hands with a towel. "You might need to go to the city if you want to get anywhere. This little town isn't going to help you get live gigs. What do you play? Bass?"

"I play the ukelele," she answered. "And I sing. There are two of us in the band. We're sort of folk rock, alternative."

Helen nodded. "That sounds lovely. I myself can't sing a note, so I really respect those who can. My voice gets a lot of use for other things."

"Thank you." Esther assumed she meant making small talk while doing people's hair and makeup.

"When I first came to England, I used to work in a hospital in London as a healthcare assistant. It wasn't a great job for me, but I managed to stick it out for a few years." She swallowed and passed her hand over her forehead. "Anyway, that's not the point. The point is that I decided I'd suck it up and re-train. I had always wanted to be a makeup artist and open my own business. I got onto a good wicket doing weddings. Some people spend a lot of money on that one day."

Hair spray came towards Esther's face in a shot of foul-tasting mist.

"Good on you," Esther said, when she felt it was safe to talk again.

"That was a really hard time, because I've got four kids. Their dad was in and out of jobs. It was a year of beans on toast. A roast beef stretched for almost a week. We made do." She shook her head.

Esther let out a low whistle.

"But it was absolutely worth it. So, my message to you is keep pushing for what you want to do. Don't get stuck. Don't stop moving."

"That's good advice. But I just don't see the appeal of the big cities. Spending all your money on rent and a long daily commute?" Esther asked.

"Some don't have a choice, though. There just aren't that many jobs. It shouldn't even be an issue these days, really, should it? We should all be able to work from anywhere with remote work, video calling and all of that. You could play your songs on social media, you know."

"Oh, I definitely agree. How did you end up in Ledstow then?" Esther said, twitching her nose as a lock of hair fell down and tickled her nose.

"My brother lives here. He's a bit older but he's got two kids similar in age to mine. I really just wanted my children to have cousins to play with. The kids are in the rock climbing club together." She considered a moment. "Oh, and I knew poor Harding through doing makeup for the theatre groups in London. He was the one who got me into this gig. It's not paid, you know. And I owed him a favour. Well, owed him my life, really."

"Did you?" Esther asked, interest pricking.

"He helped me out with a few things back when I was

struggling. He even found me a place to live. I was so upset when I found out about him passing away."

Helen grabbed a mirror off the desk and showed her the back of the hairstyle.

"Very nice," she said.

"Excuse me." Helen covered her mouth with her hand and coughed. "Sorry about that," she said, and her voice was now much quieter, almost breathy. She changed her mind and pulled out a lock of hair to re-pin it.

Esther tried to ignore the pulling and tweaking as she thought about what Helen had said. That she owed Mr Castle her life. That was a position of power, she realized. Had he tried to collect on it one too many times? Had the debt hanging over her head become too much for Helen? Had she simply snapped?

"But you love working in theatre now?" Esther asked. "I mean, you could always quit the production if you wanted to."

"Yeah, of course I could. I work at a beauty salon here in town. This is just a labour of love."

"Good on you," Esther said, but she was thinking that there was something about Helen that she couldn't quite put a finger on. Her answers were all normal, and what she said was perfectly fine. But something screamed that this was a woman with secrets.

"I was at the funeral, Harding's funeral, today…" She said, but trailed off, curious if Helen would say anything about why she wasn't there. She looked in the mirror at the face hovering above her own.

"Oh? Was it a nice one, then?"

"Yes. One of the largest funerals I've been to. Bettina was there. And Cara was too."

"Mm." Helen's mouth was a thin line as she concentrated on what she was doing, so Esther gave up. She obviously wasn't going to give anything away.

CHAPTER 11

The next morning was the first dress rehearsal. It was held at The Cutting Theatre, instead of just at the old stonemason's hall, where they usually practised. The theatre was in the middle of town and people peered in the front windows as they passed. Prepared for a long day, Esther packed lots of snacks, including a container of biscuits that she passed around the cast, while they were waiting.

"What is this recipe?" Lee asked, a look of pure bliss on his face. "I'm not usually into sweet stuff. But this!"

"Family recipe," she said, secretly proud of how well she had made her nan's biscuits. "It all feels real now that we're at the proper theatre, doesn't it?"

Three full dress rehearsals were planned, but this was the only one at the theatre, as it was booked for the next few nights. So this was their chance to get things right for the performance and get used to the size of the space and the way the stage was oriented.

Lee shrugged. "All stages are the same to me."

"I'm hyped," Poppy said, as she sank into a lunge.

"Esther?" A man with greying hair at the temples called her name, then led her over to a rack full of costumes. It smelt of mothballs. He reached in and pulled out a dress, grunting as he lifted it up. "Straight ahead."

Small cubicles had been curtained off and she walked in.

"Put this on. Yell out when you get to the fastenings."

She lifted it up and felt an ache through her shoulders. The dress was much heavier than she expected. When she had it mostly on, she called out. The face that appeared at the curtain had darkish brown skin and beautiful eyes. She fussed with the hooks.

"Hello, are you new to the group? I'm Nadine." Her voice was silky soft.

"Yes, I am. In fact, I'm pretty new to all of this. How do you know what size to make the costumes?"

"We asked for measurements early on. I think you're wearing the dress that was meant for Cara."

"Oh, right. And if it doesn't fit?" Esther asked, as Nadine pulled the sides in roughly.

"Well, I can let it out if need be. We have some time. I can work fast. Arms out."

Esther lifted her arms obediently as Nadine pulled the sleeves down and examined the length with a critical eye. With a start, she remembered that she needed to question these people and racked her brain for something to start off a casual conversation.

"How did you get into this?"

"My husband and I made the costumes for a medieval re-enactment that Bettina was part of, and she somehow convinced us from there. There was a lot of wine involved. And we're still here, I guess."

"So, who has been the worst person to dress from the cast?"

"Oh, good question. Without a doubt, it was Harding. God rest his soul, of course."

"Of course," Esther murmured.

"He did look dashing in some of the outfits, even though he was an older gentleman."

"You leave us older gentlemen alone," the man from before said, popping in and putting an affectionate arm around Nadine's waist.

"You've met Oliver, my husband?" Nadine asked. "I was just telling her about how Harding was so impatient that he wouldn't let anyone adjust his costume. He would be talking on his mobile while getting dressed. He also didn't like people going near his feet. So he often ended up wearing his own shoes on the stage." Nadine shook her head, scandalised. "And his own socks!"

"Hmm, that's not good," Esther said, since it seemed like a response was needed.

Nadine came towards her with pins in her mouth, pulling one out to pin the sleeve up. She unrolled the measuring tape, quickly and skilfully circling it around Esther's chest.

"He was just used to getting what he wanted," Oliver said. "He was alright, really."

"We need a bit extra around the bust and the sleeves taken up," Nadine said, making a note of the numbers on a scrap of paper. "I'll have that sorted for you."

"Thank you."

Esther went back to the seats to wait, pondering the enigma that was Harding Castle.

"You're coming?" Roman pointed at her with a pen. "I'm organising the wrap party and I've been told we can't just serve sausage rolls and samosas. It needs to be fancier than that. Do you have any allergies or preferences?"

"Um…"

"So far, we've got two gluten free, one celiac, one vegan and… a peanut allergy. No, that one was Harding, sorry. I'll cross that off." He put a line through it and then looked up at her. "That wasn't very sensitive, was it?"

"It's alright."

"Are you bringing a plus one? Just for the catering. So we know how many people we need food for."

"I'm not," she said, smiling at him. He seemed so young. "How old are you, Roman?"

"Twenty. Would you know if any of the other ladies are bringing a plus one?" He paused. "Like Poppy?"

Smooth, Esther thought. "No, I don't. You should ask her."

"I thought it might save time."

"Just ask her, Roman. You never know what she'll say."

THEY WERE DRESSED and had their makeup done early. Then there was a lot of waiting around in the seats, while Bettina and Lee organised the sound and lighting crew. Esther rubbed her hands together, both to warm them and because she was excited. Nervous energy kept her from standing still.

"How cute is this?" Esther asked, looking around at the upper stalls, which were decorated to look like an old-fashioned theatre. A stage was surrounded with chairs on three sides.

"Only eighty seats. And we'll be lucky to fill those," Bettina snapped, walking past, dialling a number on her phone.

"Haven't you been here before?" Cara asked. "They have comedy shows on here sometimes." She lowered her voice and jerked her head at Bettina's retreating back. "She'll only get worse as it leads up to opening night."

"Is she always like this?"

"Pretty much. I've made prompts for you in case you forget your lines," Cara said. "Otherwise, I'm just going to sit here and read my book, unless anyone needs me."

"Thank you," she said, opening up the script to read over it again. "What are you reading?"

"The Wildlife of Somerset Through Time. Non-fiction, although it could almost be a romance novel title," she laughed.

"Do you read romance?"

"I read everything," Cara said. "I'm so lucky to work in a library. Historical. Manga. Memoirs. Science fiction. Historical romance. Some of the romance novels I've read have the greatest insight into human nature and relationships."

"That's so true. They get such a bad wrap, though."

Cara nodded. "They do."

Esther was able to meet Clark outside while they were waiting. He watched her intently as she came around the corner.

"Where are you at with the investigation?" she asked, because his intense stare made her feel like she'd forgotten to put on clothes.

"I've been fighting to get a coroner's report," he said. "Because Castle had high blood pressure, it's difficult to get anyone to suspect anything other than natural causes."

"Right."

"We should get the results soon."

"There is no one here who really hated acting with him, but he sounds like an unpleasant sort, generally. Not many people liked him, that's for sure. He seems to have annoyed people in many different ways."

"Yes, you're right." He frowned. "But we have to find the reason big enough for murder." He leaned back against the oak tree. "We're a bit stuck with the case at the moment. But I have been working on finding this Chase Russell to help Mick out. Remember how I said I'd let you know about the register at Dot's? Well, it showed that Chase Russell had booked accommodation from the start to the end of January, but he completely disappeared last week. That's two weeks early. It was a twin room. After she rang Mick, the guy threatened her."

"So she didn't want to tell us about it." Esther thought back to Dot, with her rockstar style, and something tugged at her subconscious. "The wheels," she said, slowly. "Dot couldn't be the mysterious 'Rock 'n Roll 68' from your dream email, could she?"

"I don't know, Esther. But it could be worth a try."

"Definitely. Also, Helen, the hair and makeup lady, is pretty suspicious. She knew Harding from earlier and mentioned that she owed him her life. Perhaps he took advantage of that?"

"A few things to think about." Clark was opening and closing his hands and seemed distracted.

"Are you alright?"

"I'm not all that comfortable with acting."

"Really? But you're a lecturer. Don't you speak in front of hundreds of bored students? You have to interview people at the police station. You tackle criminals!"

He laughed softly. "Those are different."

"Well, you once showed me a way to relax and focus. Having anxiety, I've developed a few different tricks, so maybe I can help you. I realized that music helped me to feel like a different person. A bouncy track with a stonking beat fills me with energy and strength. But it was only recently that I found out I didn't need to actually listen to the music. I could sing the song to myself and I'd get the same results. So think of a song that gets you amped. Your song. Have you got one?"

He nodded.

"You don't have to tell me what it is. Sing it as loud as you can inside your head." She thought of her own song, and boogied for a second in a little micro-dance. "You can use it as a soundtrack and imagine yourself as the main character of a movie."

Clark smiled.

"Did it help?"

"Yeah, I'll try it. Thanks."

It seemed as if he was going to come towards her to kiss her before he went back in, but he lightly brushed her hand instead and went up the steps. One of these times she was going to plant a smooch on his face.

"Do you normally hang out with the cast much?" Esther asked Cara, between scenes. She pulled out a ham sandwich.

"Not outside of rehearsals, usually. Until the wrap party, of course. Aren't you sick of us yet?" She looked at her watch. "Ooh, I've got work in half an hour. It's always hard to get anyone at the library on a Saturday."

"Well, it's just that Scottie just opened his new restaurant. I wonder if we should go along there sometime this week and support him." Esther was quite proud of her idea. Mix a nosy witch with some food and drink and some secrets might just get spilled.

"That's not a bad idea," Cara said.

"I'll message the group chat," Esther replied. "We need some downtime too."

CHAPTER 12

Esther spent the rest of the day talking to herself as she repeated her lines. In the evening, she put her hair up in a bun and changed into her purple shirt and jeans, and looked at herself in the mirror.

"What? Yes, I do go out, occasionally," she said to Louis, who could give the grumpiest of cats a run for their money with his death stare.

She arrived at Clark's house and knocked on the door. He lived in the middle of a row of Georgian-style flats with large windows, with a neat garden bed on either side of the front steps. She wondered what his family would be like. Would they be as serious as him? Would they bring up that she and Clark had met while he was questioning her as a witness?

"Evening. I'm Owen," said the man who opened the door.

Esther blinked. It was a good insight into how Clark would look in twenty years or so; the same height, keen eyes and ready smile. Owen's hair was thinning at the front and silver lined his short beard.

"Nice to meet you," she said.

"Come in. Come in." He put his hands out to take her coat and she shrugged it off. "Clark's through here, in the kitchen. The bathroom is that way."

Esther walked through into the lounge. A girl was sitting on the couch and she ignored her as Esther walked past to where she could see Clark wrestling with a huge crock pot.

"Hi," he said, sitting it carefully on a trivet and lifting the lid off. Wondrous smells of spices and chicken and clouds of steam billowed up. He waved the steam away from his face. "You're right on time."

"That smells amazing."

He gave it a stir and put the pot back in, closing the door carefully. Then he ushered her into the lounge. He reached over and tousled the girl's hair, and she swatted at his hand.

"Triss, this is Esther. And you met Dad? I've just got to go and sort out the vegetables."

"He's been planning the meal out all day." Triss rolled her eyes. "So you two are acting together? That's random." Triss moved a headphone off her ear and looked up at Esther from the couch. The dye in her hair had faded a lot from the photo on the dashboard.

"Yeah, it is a bit," admitted Esther, taking a seat in the armchair. She assumed that Clark hadn't told Triss about the murder investigation. "We are having a good time, though. What are you listening to?"

Triss had light hair, big eyes and fine features. She didn't look a lot like Clark or her dad, except she had the same nose. Esther thought she must resemble their mother.

"It's the latest Taylor Swift. Not off her album but it was something she released just for the fans, and it's so good. Clark said you're in a band?"

"Yes, with my friend, Ashton. Our name is Soulful. Just the two of us."

"Anything I'd know?"

"No, probably not. It's folk rock. So far, we've mostly played at retirement homes. But we want to do some more live performances."

"I've got some really old songs in my playlist, like the original *Sound of Silence* by Simon & Garfunkel and *Get Together* by The Youngbloods. Do you know those?"

"Good choices." Esther smiled, but the 'really old' part made her feel like she had one foot in the grave.

The girl nodded. "Do you play chess?"

"Badly. Do you?"

"I'm in the chess club at school. Would you 'verse' me?"

"Don't try and catch her out, kiddo," Clark said, coming through with a plate full of steaming potatoes, which he placed on the table. He spoke out of the side of his mouth. "She is really good. Beats me half the time now."

Triss rolled her eyes. "More than half the time."

"Okay, well, I probably don't have much chance, then. I'd feel more confident in playing Cluedo. Do you have that?"

"After tea, eh?" Clark asked.

"Wine?" asked Owen. "I'll be your waiter tonight," he said, with a flourish.

"Just a little, thanks."

"Funniest looking waiter I've seen," Clark said.

They had a lovely dinner, where Owen talked about his time spent living in Spain.

"I was just near Barcelona. Have you been there?"

"No, I haven't."

"Dad's always talking about it. I reckon he should go back."

Owen looked over at his son, as if this was a conversation they'd had many times. "Clark can be a bit of a stick in the mud. That's why I was so surprised when he took this job and moved towns. I've known a few academics in my time and they don't normally take many risks. His mother, Selene, was a professor of Ancient Languages, you see."

"I think it was all her talk of the Egyptians that got me interested in learning about the unexplained. She used to tell me bedtime stories. We know so much about them but we know so little about them at the same time."

"I was the more adventurous one of the two of us," Owen said. "I was actually in Spain when she passed away. That's why Triss ended up living with Clark here. Then I lost my job because I got sick, so it made financial sense."

Esther looked at him with sympathy. It must be a hard topic to talk about, but he chatted openly with the others, as if they were all used to discussing it.

"Dad only lives round the corner," Triss said. "We see him a lot."

Owen nodded. "What do your parents do, Esther? Or are they retired?"

"Dad is an accountant and my mother is a judge." She said the last part really quietly. She wanted to be honest with these people, but didn't want the inevitable fuss made.

"Oh wow, like *Judge Judy*?" Triss asked.

Esther sighed. "A little bit, yeah."

"That is impressive," Owen said. "What was it like growing up with a judge in the house? I bet you had to be squeaky clean. No smoking behind the bike sheds?"

"Pretty much." She smiled, because that was actually spot on.

"That must have been hard on you. I bet she couldn't ever talk about what she was working on either."

Esther nodded. "There were definitely a few silences around the dining table."

"We talk about everything here. How's your wee boyfriend?" he asked Triss.

"He's away on a skiing holiday. Back next week."

Owen nodded. "Clark tells me you're a really good singer?"

"He's very kind," she said, feeling her cheeks grow a little warm.

"Well no. He is usually pretty spot on. So if he says you're great at something, then you should probably own it, love."

"Don't worry about Owen." Clark smiled. "I think you get to a certain age and you think you can say whatever you like."

"That's ok," she said.

Owen winked at her.

"The chicken was delicious," she said. But it was the wholesome, chaotic feel of the meal that she most appreciated.

In her family, meals always had an expectation that came with them, that she privately called the 'ta-da effect', where the recipe was the latest trend in cooking or the kids were expected to talk about their amazing exam result. Sometimes, their meal was food her mother had been gifted as a thanks for her volunteer work. Their conversations were almost scripted. Everything had to be the best.

"That one is the boy's top recipe." Owen stacked up their plates and clattered the cutlery on top.

"Yeah, we eat a lot of pasta, normally," Triss added.

"We do." Clark stood up. "For dessert, I've just got ice cream. Is that going to be alright?"

"That's perfect," she said.

"I'll go and see Dot again," Clark said to her, as he came back with a bowl filled with round scoops of ice cream, covered in chocolate sauce. "It's worth a try. Although, the email, if it was her, seems really out of character. She's one of the strongest people I've met."

"There must be a reason."

When she finished scraping the chocolate ice cream from the bottom of the bowl, Clark took the dish.

"I'll walk her out," he said to his family.

"Bye," Triss said.

"It was lovely to meet you, Esther." Owen gave her a wave from the kitchen.

He helped her into her coat and shut the door behind them. "Did you have a nice time tonight?"

"Yeah, I did. Your family are really good people. Oh, I did say we were going to play Cluedo..." She didn't want to let Triss down, especially not when she'd just met her. It felt a little like he was rushing her out.

"I've been waiting a long time to do this," Clark said, advancing on her. His arm came around her neck to the back of her head to tilt her face up.

But Esther stopped him. "What are you doing? You've been doing the friend zone dance for the last couple of weeks!"

"Friend zone?" he asked, looking genuinely puzzled. He scratched his head. "No way. We've talked most days. I was just waiting for you to meet my girl. Triss is extremely possessive of me, so I didn't want to rush into anything until I knew that there wasn't going to be any barriers. You passed muster with her. Now, I'm rushing," he said.

Esther eyed him. "Just tell me, next time. I thought you'd gone off me."

"You thought... I've been staring at you every minute we're together. It's quite distracting when we're rehearsing."

"I'm distracting?" she whispered. "I'm distracting?"

They stood, staring at each other from a foot apart, then dived into the kiss at the same moment, both going the same way. Their noses collided painfully.

Clark reached out and gently rubbed her nose with his fingers, then gave it a light peck. "Are you alright?"

She nodded. A twitch of the curtains alerted her that

someone was wondering what was taking so long, and she thought it must be Triss.

"She's really cool," Esther said. "You and your dad have done a great job with her. I wish I was like her when I was that age."

He curled his arm around her shoulders, as they walked towards her car. It was parked under a tree over the other side of the road and was a dark spot.

"She has her moments. Don't think it's all plain sailing."

"I bet. But you've got such a great wee family," she said. "Thanks for introducing me."

"Not so fast," he said. "I meant it." He stepped in close and his other arm held her still, while he brought his lips towards hers, then stopped, teasing. His lips gently landed on her jaw line, gradually tickling as he kissed closer to her mouth. He leaned in and pressed her against the side of the car, her whole body feeling the heat of him. "You looked so happy tonight. And when you got that cute little blush…"

A cat jumped off the car beside them and ran over the driveway. Harsh security lights flicked on and flooded them with light.

Clark stuck his hands in his pockets like a guilty teenager. "I'll see you tomorrow," he said.

CHAPTER 13

The next day, in the hall, Clark deigned to give Esther a quick grin and a press of the hand as they passed each other on the way to the dressing rooms. Wow, she thought. Was she so starved for affection that a smile got her heart racing?

Moran was sitting at the piano, and she went over to him.

"You are really gifted at songwriting," she said to him. "I love the melodies, and the way you've integrated the original script and more modern language in the lyrics."

"I've been working on this for a few years. I'm just lucky Mrs V wanted to take a chance on me."

"Can I give you some feedback?"

"Why not? Go ahead."

"There's just one part, where I think you should go

into A minor, before going to F. At the very end of 'What Kind of Love?'"

He put his hands on the keys, and tried it out. The new progression sounded perfect to Esther's ear.

Moran grinned and used his pen to make a note. "I think you'll do alright," he said.

There was a scene in which Clark had to stand an arm's length in front of her as they acted out a domestic afternoon. At one point, he had struggled with a line, and Bettina clicked her tongue. Remembering that he wasn't comfortable and that she'd basically forced him into the play, she reached out and lightly stroked the little finger of his hand where it hung by his side.

After the practise, Bettina called Lee and Clark over. "I'm going to get Lee to learn these lines, too. He can be the understudy, in case of anything happening. Is that all fine?"

"I pretty much know them, already," Lee said, and flashed his teeth.

"Excuse me," Helen said, tapping her shoulder. "I'd like to make a change to the way I do your makeup tonight."

"Me?" Esther asked.

Helen nodded. "Do you mind coming here at, say, six?"

"Sure. That's no problem."

Helen said goodbye in her soft, hoarse voice and seemed to almost glide down the hall. Esther watched her go. This was her chance to question her fully about the night of the murder.

♫

WHEN SHE LEFT THE HALL, she caught up with Clark. The street was lined with old stone walls with bushes flowing over the top. In spring, they would burst into flower, making a colourful sight.

"You've got your own understudy. Fancy," she said. "We must be real actors, now."

"Me? Hardly. I don't know why Bettina agreed to let me in the play. She's a real stickler for perfection, otherwise."

"Yes," she said, quickly. "She must have her reasons. By the way, we should talk to the original understudies," she said. "It's a bit strange that they both quit, don't you think?"

"Oh, yes, I did have that in my notes," he said. "They would have been the prime suspects, otherwise. With the leading man and lady out of the way, they could jump right into the starring roles. Yes, let's hunt them down. We'll just say we're touching base as we take on the new roles."

"Don't say you're hunting them down. You'll scare them off."

"Well, I will have to look into the case files to find their details."

"I've got a quick shift at the music shop this afternoon, but I'll meet you after. Say 3:30?"

"That works for me," he said.

GRETA GREEN WAS like one of the stars of old Hollywood. She had a sort of 1920's grace, with long, gently curling brown hair and one pale arm draped elegantly over the back of the chair. Her eyes were half-closed as she watched her cat stretch out on the floor.

"She looks like hard work," Clark said, from outside the door. "I'll leave this one to you."

"Thanks," Esther said, wryly. But he'd already turned away. Luckily, Greta turned out to be easy to talk to. Noticing the cover of the book she was reading, Esther asked her whether it was good.

"It's pretty racy," she said. "My grandmother got me into reading romance novels. She used to let me borrow hers when I was only about eleven or twelve. My mum and dad never noticed. Grandparents are delicious, aren't they?"

"I have a great relationship with my nan," Esther agreed. "Sudoku puzzles are her thing. Anyway, I wanted to see if there's anything I need to know about the cast or…"

"I left due to professional differences with Mrs V," she said. "Just do everything she says and you'll be fine," she said, rather bitterly.

"What exactly did you disagree over? Just so that we can be aware."

"Oh, tea cups, of all things. Because we weren't acting most of the time, I ended up doing everyone's dishes each day. I think there were around sixteen people who, on average, had two hot drinks a day. The one day I put my foot down and decided not to do them, Bettina made a fuss. But that was the final straw. We'd been disagreeing on things since we met. Then, of course, Freddy left too."

"Ah, right. Why do you say, 'of course'?"

"Ask him yourself. I'll fetch him."

Esther looked around at the living room while she waited. Greta came out arm in arm with a stocky middle-aged man. He had a huge beard and light, brown skin. "He convinced me to start a YouTube channel with him."

"It makes the channel a bit more appetising having this one on there," he said. His voice was surprisingly deep and sonorous, and Esther could see that he would make a great actor. "It's called Voice and Virtue, if you want to look it up. We talk about focus for creatives."

"We've only made nine videos and Freddy's already

got a contact for some advertising work and I'm going to record an audiobook for a publisher."

"Oh, great news. How did you get into acting in the first place?" she asked.

"With a voice like mine, how could I do anything else?" Freddy boomed.

"I think she was talking to me," Greta said, "if you don't mind." She aimed a sweet smile at Freddy.

"Sorry darling."

"I just fell into it really. I was picked up to do some modelling and then I started doing bit parts. They always told me I was so pretty — so pretty — until I got to a certain age and they stopped saying that quite so often. But I felt like the same person on the inside, you know? I came back home to Ledstow and took up photography, then I could show others how beautiful they are on the inside."

"Very different from my story."

"Yes, a little different."

"I used to be a radio announcer, if you can believe that. I only started acting to impress a lady."

Esther's eyes flicked to Greta.

"No, not her. Her name was Jameela." The name sounded beautiful in Freddy's voice. "It's all about my Greta now, though."

"And you two hit it off during rehearsals?"

Greta looked at Freddy and nodded. "There was a lot of waiting around as understudies."

"We were literally in the shadow of Harding and Cara. Just waiting in the wings."

"That must have made you frustrated."

Greta looked surprised. "No, that's just the way of it. We're actually grateful as we wouldn't have gotten to know each other otherwise. We quit because we realised that—" She paused.

Freddy continued. "We're only young once. Instead of waiting around to maybe play a part if we are needed, we are heading off on a holiday. Flights to Italy booked. Nothing can stop us now." Freddy pointed to the corner of the room where a black suitcase was waiting.

"We actually have one of the cast to thank for that, too. One of the young ones, Poppy, said that we don't have to do the play just because we feel a sense of duty."

"Well, you two have a good holiday," Esther said, standing up and putting her bag on. "Thank you for being so open with me. You don't know me from a bar of soap, after all."

"We're happy to let you know what you're in for. And if you're someone who can get along with some really big personalities, you'll be fine."

Esther got into the car, where Clark was waiting, reading an email on his phone.

"Alright, that's two we can tick off the list," she said, getting in. "They were such lovely people."

"Two?" Clark moved his arm from where it was hanging across the back of her seat.

"Mm. Both Freddy and Greta were there. It seems like they're in a relationship. They're heading out of the country in a few days."

Clark frowned. "Surely, that makes them more suspicious?"

"Oh, right. It does sound bad, doesn't it? But they are the warmest people. And so open. I just didn't get that vibe from them."

"Not a lot we can do about it since it's not strictly a murder case, anyway. I can't stop them from leaving."

Esther worried at her lip, thinking she should have asked more questions. It did seem like something guilty people would do. Why was she going off vibes? Could she trust her intuition?

"Well, I ended up checking my emails while I was waiting for you," he said. "The findings from the coroner came back. Harding had a huge sudden heart rate spike. There was no poison substance found. The preliminary notes said that it was most likely consistent with a heart attack. It almost seems like he was frightened to death."

"Frightened of what, though?" she asked, under her breath.

He turned the key. "Exactly. Do you have time to pop

into Dot's with me? It's easier if I do it now."

"Alright. Then I have to meet Helen."

They drove to the Gatehouse and parked in an expensive onstreet park.

"Hello Dot," Clark said, as he pushed open the door. "It's me."

"Young 'un," she said. "I didn't think you'd be back so soon."

"Do you know anything about this?" He pulled out a printed copy of the email he'd told her about. One line of writing was printed in black font at the top. She stood up out of her wheelchair to look at it closer.

She put one hand on the front of the desk. "You finally figured it out, did you? But I can't talk about this."

"Why not?"

She beckoned to him to come closer. "I was warned, in no uncertain terms."

"If you're worried about Chase, he's gone. No one's seen him at all."

She shook her head.

Clark frowned.

But Esther remembered how Dot had used clues the last time. "It's alright, Dot. I get it. But just know that I work in the music shop here, and I always love chatting to customers."

Dot sat back down in her chair, her face impassive. "See you later."

CHAPTER 14

When Esther arrived, Helen was sipping a cup of tea. The classical music was up loud and she leant forward to turn it down.

"I'm sorry," she said. "I often get this tinnitus, you know, ringing in the ears, and it stops me from being able to concentrate on things. But there doesn't seem to be much the doctors can do about it. The music helps a little."

"I completely understand. It can be difficult if you feel like no one's listening to you."

Helen settled her tea cup in its saucer. "I was expecting you. It's just that I get so lost in the music, sometimes." She sat up straighter and reached for her makeup palette. "Sit down, sit down. Get comfortable.

Bettina was complaining that you don't look pale enough. So I wanted to try a slightly different colour. Is that going to be ok?"

"Gosh, she really is a perfectionist." Esther said, before pressing her lips together so makeup didn't go in her mouth.

Helen finished applying the cool creme foundation to Esther's face and leaned back.

"Oh, but she's good. That's why we're all here, I guess." Helen put the brushes down and reached for her cup, which was empty. "Oh, I don't feel that great," she said, stumbling a bit. "Excuse me. Oh, I've got to—"

Helen turned away, and a brain-curdling scream erupted from her mouth. She crumpled to the ground. It seemed to go on forever, drilling into Esther's skull.

Esther put both hands over ears, as the noise went on, pressing hard to get that siren sound out of her mind. She couldn't move, couldn't think. Finally, it subsided to a wailing sob, and Esther went to her, kneeling down on the wooden floor. How long had the sound gone on? One minute? Five?

She patted Helen's shoulder, as she struggled to sit up again, and her face was as pale as if she was the one in the white cream foundation.

"Are you alright? What happened?"

Helen was breathing fast, but she didn't seem to be struggling.

Her words came softly. "Danger. Nearby. Coming."

"What's the matter? I'll call an ambulance."

But Helen grabbed her hand in her cool one. She shook her head. "No, please. No ambulance. It's not me. You."

♫

"I THINK I MET A BANSHEE." That was a sentence that Esther never thought she'd say.

She had dropped in to see her nan after the incident with Helen, since the nursing home wasn't far from the hall. It smelt of that same mixture of cooking and tea as it always did. She leaned in to cuddle her grandmother, inhaling her perfume that always took her straight back to childhood, then dropped into the chair with a sigh.

"Blue Eyes," her nan said, leaning forward. "Lovely to see you."

That was when Esther dropped her bombshell, and leaned back to see what her grandmother thought.

Hope's blue eyes sparkled. "Well, why not? Tell me more about it."

"Really? Have you ever met a banshee?"

"No, I have not. But, knowing what we know about our wee town, it's not that improbable, darling. Tell me what happened."

"Okay, well, the makeup and hair lady for the production, Helen Doyle, just started screaming when I was with her. Screeching, really, as if she couldn't stop it. And she said that I was in danger. I stayed with her until she calmed down, but I didn't pry too much. She said she was perfectly fine."

"She said you were in danger?" Hope looked concerned.

"I'm not really worried about that," Esther said. "But there was something so otherworldly about that scream. As if it was coming from some other place than inside Helen. It was awful. I think it was her scream we heard the other night."

Hope raised her eyebrows in surprise. "That makes sense, lovely."

"There's more. I wondered if, perhaps, that scream had been enough to frighten Harding to death."

"This is the lawyer? Well, that would mean that, for one thing — she held up a gnarled finger — Helen, our banshee, was in the neighbourhood on the night of the crime. And secondly, that the scream, that was warning of Harding's own death, killed him."

"Yes," Esther said, slowly. "I guess it would. But I'm sure that most people in Ledstow would have heard that scream."

"The scream heralding his own death killed him. Strange. But not impossible."

Esther noticed that her grandmother leaned her head

back on the chair and closed her eyes, briefly. She leaned forward.

"How are you doing, nan? Have you been joining in any of the activities?"

She answered with her eyes closed. "Oh, yes, now and then. Kevin makes me."

"I like the sound of this Kevin. He seems like a good sort."

Hope opened one eye and fixed it on her. "He'll be here shortly. There's bingo on tonight. It's on every week. You could come along if you want to."

"What time? You aren't going to be raging it up all night, are you?"

"Oh, I think it starts at 6:30. Dinner is all over and done with by then. It's ridiculous, really."

Esther nodded. "I will join you, then. Ridiculous is my theme of the month."

Her nan smiled. "I might have a quick nap, first."

Esther settled in, comfortably. "Sure. I can read my book."

WITH HELP FROM HOPE, Esther managed to get some cheese on toast for dinner, while the residents ate their roast pork and Yorkshire pudding.

Her grandmother warned her that bingo wouldn't be

like they had played in school to learn their numbers, but Esther was still shocked. The game was so fast-paced that Esther struggled to keep track of the numbers, especially as each one had a code.

"Clickety click. Buttered scone." The caller rattled them off in a practised voice as if he was commentating a race.

Hope had an impassive smile on her face. It was almost like the stream of digits didn't affect her at all.

"Line," someone yelled, and it seemed to Esther as if there was hardly time. They'd only just started.

"Man alive." The caller said. "Duck and a crutch. Twenty seven."

At one point, Kevin switched bingo boards with Hope as she had stamped more squares. Esther raised her eyebrows but Hope only laughed and slid his one back across.

"He doesn't like it because I always win."

"She cheats," Kevin said, with a laugh.

"Bingo," Hope called a few moments later, a triumphant look on her face.

Esther had to admit that she really enjoyed it. It was a welcome escape from the secrets, pretending and suspicion that the rest of her life had become.

Did everyone have so many secrets? Was it because they were actors? Or was it just this particular group of people?

They'd found out a lot, but it seemed that they weren't much closer to an answer, so Esther racked her brains for ways to get to know some of the cast and crew better. They were running out of time until the show.

145

CHAPTER 15

"I tried calling you last night," Clark said, when he arrived at her flat in the morning with two takeaway coffees. He kissed her on the cheek, his stubble grazing her skin.

"Oh, I saw that. I was playing bingo with my grandmother," she said.

"How was that?"

"It was great. Took my mind off everything," she said. "Then I was pretty tired after that. Never underestimate an older person, I tell you."

"I never would. I've been schooled by too many," he joked.

"Have a seat," she said, although he was already pulling out a chair. It gave her a tiny warm feeling that he was comfortable enough at her place to do that.

"This has been the most full on two weeks," he said. I actually can't wait until it's over. What would you be doing if we weren't doing the play?"

"Probably watching musicals, like *Hamilton* or *Mamma Mia*. Or reading my book. I do want to start writing my own songs, too. I'd like to give it a try, anyway. What about you?"

"I'd take Triss down to netball. Work on my research. And I'd take you out on some really romantic dates."

"Oh yeah. What did you have in mind?"

"Well, to be honest, you probably know Ledstow better than me. But I think you'd like to go to dinner and then the theatre."

She narrowed her eyes. "It's an A plus for you, professor," she said. "Don't forget we are going out for dinner tonight at Scottie's new place."

He put his coffee down, and walked to the middle of the room. "Yes," he said. "With the whole crew. We should make a plan for questioning people. But first, let's just run through that one scene."

THE RESTAURANT WAS DIMLY LIT and trendy. Esther could already tell it had a great atmosphere. She made a beeline for Cara, who was standing at the bar.

"Esther! This is Abe. He just arrived from, ah, overseas."

The man smiled and said, "Hello", which made Esther feel like the sun was shining on her. He was a head taller than her and he was really solid, with long dark hair. He was one of the most beautiful men she'd ever seen.

She pulled her eyes away from him, as Bettina came over. "Darlings, we are absolutely positively going to make this show shine. Look at all of you beautiful things!"

"The table's ready," Scottie said. They followed him into a private enclave which was surrounded by windows.

"I'm so impressed," Esther said to him, as they were standing by the table waiting to take their place. "The place looks great."

"Yes," Poppy said, appearing from nowhere at her side. "It's so cool. Sorry I was late. I just came from work."

"What *do* you do for a job?" Esther asked. She had never heard Poppy mention working before. She'd assumed she was unemployed or studying.

"Oh, sort of pest control," she said. "I used to be a nurse but I needed something more flexible."

Esther took a breath to ask another question, but Poppy had turned away, already chatting to someone else. Clark arrived then and waved to her from the other side of the table.

"I'll take Lee," he whispered as he leaned in to kiss her cheek. "You take Bettina."

"No way. Can we swap? She loves you."

Clark sighed. "Fine."

Esther made sure to sit between Lee and Bettina so she could hear what was going on.

When they were all sitting down, Scottie stood next to Esther and lifted his arms. "Welcome to Meat Around the Grill. A love affair with meat," he said, with a flourish of his arm. "This is my first adventure into owning a restaurant. I have very little idea what I'm doing," he said, with a laugh. "But I can cook."

"What a relief," Bettina called, wiping her hand across her head, and a few people laughed.

"I've taken care of some bottles of wine. Anything after that is up to you. I'll leave you in the care of my capable wait staff."

"Good on you," Lee called. Bettina clapped. One young man walked around the table and poured out wine.

"So, Lee, will your family be coming to the production?" Esther asked him, after they had ordered.

"They have been to one or two. But I don't think they are coming to this one."

"Oh, that's a shame. Something more important on?"

"My brother's a lawyer and he has a big case on at the

moment, so he'll be working really long hours. And my parents would only come if he does."

"It sounds like you're a close family. Does he work here in town?"

"Yes, it's a small firm. Browne and Castle."

She waited until the waiter had placed their meals down, then leaned forward, ignoring the savoury smells of the food.

"He worked with Harding?"

He nodded. "Yes. He left a really big gap for them to fill. Mr Castle was a very hard-working man."

Esther pondered for a while, eating her beef and eggplant skewer. She suddenly thought of something that Lee might know about. "What happened when the understudies left? Was it a bad fight?"

"No, it wasn't bad." Lee shook his head. "Bettina likes to make everything seem dramatic but she forgets about things straight after. She is actually a really loyal and hardworking person."

Bettina stood up and lifted up her glass. "Can we all lift our glasses to my dear friend, Harding? Being around him was like being close to the sun. You knew it wasn't great but you couldn't look away. You ended up getting pulled into his orbit."

"I'm proud to have called him a mate," Scottie added.

"He would have wanted us to keep going with the show," Bettina agreed. "One more rehearsal to get it perfect, everyone. For Harding." She sat down, and Esther noticed that her eyes were shining.

"Is it normally all the same people who are part of the production?" Esther asked Lee, in a whisper.

"Bettina has been running it for as long as I've been here. I think she got Harding involved. Cara has been around for a while and so has Helen. The others are all new."

She rubbed her temples. Did that mean someone new was likely to be the murderer since that was their plan? Or was it someone who had worked with Harding before who had finally snapped?

Clark asked if she wanted to leave soon after. "Are you ready to go? You looked like you had a headache. I'll walk you home."

"No, I guess my mind is just not used to holding this much information at once. How did you go?" she asked, as they walked down the street.

"Well, the steak was beautifully cooked. Just tender, a little bit rare."

She nudged him gently with her elbow. "I mean, with the suspects."

"Remind me not to swap with you next time," Clark said drily. "Mrs V told me about some of her past lovers who are celebrities."

"Should I ask?"

"No, you shouldn't. In some detail, I might add. Also,

it turns out that Bettina lives over the road from Harding."

"Ooh," she said.

"Yes. That does put her in a convenient place for the crime. And something else. She said she'd always had a soft spot for Harding."

"Privately, I think it was more than a soft spot," Esther said. "I think it was unrequited love. Lee knew Harding outside of the play as well. His older brother worked with him at the law firm."

"Did he?" Clark sounded surprised, but seemed to second guess himself. "It's a small town. It hardly means anything."

"True." Esther tried to imagine what it would be like working with an over-achieving well-known actor of old. Only one of them had their name on the door. If Harding had made partner and Lee's brother hadn't, that could be a powerful motive for revenge. "That's a connection that we might need to investigate, though."

"Yes. The situation as far as I can tell, is this. Lee may have a motive. Helen may have a motive. Bettina had the opportunity. Greta and Freddy look suspicious as heck—"

"No way," she put in.

"And Wendy Castle still looks the most suspicious of all."

CHAPTER 16

The next morning, Clark called while she was still in bed.

"What's the time?" she asked him, voice groggy from sleep.

"Um, six thirty."

"Nope. I'm hanging up now," she said. "The cat brought a bird inside last night at around midnight and Jay attacked it. The cat, I mean."

"Oh, sorry about that," he said. "But just wait a minute. It's about Lee. I looked him up in our system. His father recently got a huge tax bill and applied for a loan but was declined. It could be unrelated, but you said that his brother was looking to make partner at the law firm."

If the family really needed money, that could be an extra reason for revenge.

"Oh no, but I like him," she said.

"Well, we need to ask him a few questions. And we'll see how he responds. I've got his address."

"Alright, then. But let's see what he says before we start accusing anybody."

"I'll pick you up. And I'll grab us a coffee on the way."

"HI GUYS," Lee said, a while later, opening the door of his house. "Is this something about the play?"

"Good morning, Lee," Esther said. It was too early for this.

"No, it's not," Clark said, at the same time. He was dressed in casual clothes, but he put on his policeman voice. "Not about the play."

"I want to be really honest with you. We're in the play to investigate Harding's death."

His eyes darted back and forth between them. "It was just old age, wasn't it?"

"We don't think so."

"How did you get my address? And why are you questioning me?"

Clark showed him his police badge. Lee gulped, but opened the door so they could come inside. He stood awkwardly in the hallway.

There were stairs on the right hand side. The carpet

was a plush bluish grey and there was a family portrait hanging on the wall.

"We just want to ask where you were on the night that Harding Castle died. Last Saturday between 8 and 10pm."

So much for the listening and learning approach, Esther thought. She leaned back against the stair railing.

"I would not kill anyone. I don't even like laying mousetraps," he said.

"Me neither," Esther said.

"Lee, we're going to level with you. The first thing is that we know you were going to come over to see Harding at that time. We know that your brother really needed to make partner at the firm. We know that your father really needed money. We think you wanted to take revenge, on your brother's behalf."

After a short silence, in which the hall clock ticked away a full eleven seconds, Lee opened his mouth. "I'm not saying anything."

Clark stared at him, his face showing hardly any expression. Just a tiny lift of the eyebrow, to show his disdain.

"Letting us know where you were would help us rule you out," he said. "None of us want to think that it's you, mate. But your silence is making you look guilty."

"This is really embarrassing."

"Just tell us what you were doing that night," Esther added.

"She'll kill me," he almost whispered.

"Your mother?" Esther asked.

He shook his head.

"Harding's wife?"

"What? No." He took a big breath. "Bettina. I went over there to take her a supply of cigarettes, alright?"

That put him in the neighbourhood at the right time. "Everyone in the cast knows she smokes. Why the big secret?" Esther asked.

"She may seem like the boss around here. But her husband hates cigarettes with a passion, so she keeps it quiet. It started last season when we were doing Cats. I said I'd bring them for her, and she pays me very well for it. Sometimes, she asks me to go over and pretend to practise our lines but we just smoke in her garden. We are good friends."

Clark shrugged his shoulders, as if getting rid of tension. He was glad that Lee had an alibi, too. "Right."

"Okay," Esther said, struggling not to laugh. It was a very elaborate ruse. "Well, we're sorry for accusing you, then, aren't we?" She elbowed Clark.

"Huh? Yes, apologies for that," he said, looking embarrassed.

"Do you know anything else that might help us?"

Lee crossed his arms. "It pains me to say it, but I think Bettina might have more to do with this than you think."

"Why do you say that?" Clark asked.

"She had a lot of complicated feelings for him."

"I'm beginning to see that," Esther said. She didn't need to ask who he meant.

"I won't say anything more." Lee shook his head, lips pressed firmly together.

"Alright, Lee," Clark said. "Thanks for helping us out. And keep it quiet about the investigation, if you can, please."

He nodded. "So you two don't like acting?" The hurt in his eyes gave Esther a twinge of guilt. She felt like they'd betrayed the whole production.

"We do, but we also want to find the murderer."

Lee walked them out, eyes still burning into their backs as they left.

When they got in the car, Esther said, "I feel awful."

"Hey, look on the bright side. At least we got a lead," Clark said. "And an alibi to check."

"I hope it's not Bettina," Esther said.

"It has to be someone," Clark said, exasperated.

Esther was idly staring out the window, when a street name jumped out at her. She'd seen this street many times before and thought nothing of it. Russell Street was a nondescript road in the middle of Ledstow. It was a common enough surname. Was it worth checking it out?

"I don't want it to be anyone I know," she said to Clark, eventually.

"Well, you decided we should join the play. It's highly

likely to be someone we know."

She looked up at him. He was facing straight ahead and sounded annoyed, and she wondered what she'd done wrong.

LATER ON, after he dropped her home, her mind kept spinning. Maybe she had forced Clark to join the play. He'd never been as keen as her to do it. But they were getting somewhere with the case, weren't they?

She made a decision. She wasn't going to be upset. The past was the past. Instead, she was going to solve the case first.

It was a few hours later when she met Helen at the hall.

"Yes, I'm descended from the ban sidhe," Helen said, unlocking the heavy door, "but I'm afraid I'm not a very good one. I feel so much pressure that I muck it up almost every time."

"That must be so hard."

"I don't even have much of an accent any more. My old ma is still in Cork. My gift, if you can call it that, sort of comes sporadically. Especially now, with the menopause. My mother has visions and then she heralds the death. Just like we're supposed to do. But, for me, it's never been that straightforward. And now, with these hot flushes and the tinnitus I never know whether it's an episode coming on or if all of this is just normal."

"I see," Esther said, remembering the blood-curdling scream. "So it *was* you screaming on Twelfth Night."

"It was." She looked down. "I was just dropping in to give Harding's wife back her foundation. Well, she lent hers to me when I needed it and I bought one for her. When I got close, I started feeling a bit funny and I knew I was about to drop. But Harding looked out the window and saw me. As he opened the door, I started running away, but it was too late. I'd seen the vision of him on the floor and the scream started to come. I don't remember much after that. I managed to make it home and my flat-mate took one look at me and bundled me into bed. I just wish it wasn't so unpredictable. When I woke up the next day, he told me what had happened and that half the town had heard it. I decided to lay low for a few days as I thought I'd got it wrong. But when I heard about poor Harding later, I realized that it wasn't just stress. I'd done the right thing. For once."

"I can sympathise with that," Esther said, with feeling. She curled her hands into fists. "I'm not even sure when I'm doing magic or not."

Helen nodded. "I knew I sensed something of the magical about you," she said. "Are you with the coven here or practising solo?"

"It's all really new for me. Definitely flying solo.

Could I ask you some more about the night that you went to Harding's?"

"Alright, yes. Er, how come?"

"I'm looking into his death. In your vision, did you see anything about how he died?"

"No, I assumed it was heart problems. I didn't see anyone else or anything."

"Does the coven here know about you?"

"Oh yes, I told them about my vision of Harding, as soon as it happened."

That was interesting. "Who did you tell? It's alright, I know them."

Helen eyed her. "Lottie is who I told," she said, quietly. "She's always helped me when I've needed it."

Esther remembered how Lottie had looked that morning, after the scream. As if she'd been up all night.

"Okay, thanks, Helen."

"One other thing. I did see our own Cara down Beekeeper's Lane that night. I'm not sure what she was doing," she said. "Probably nothing. But she might know more about it."

"Oh, really. Are you sure it was her?"

She nodded, a quick movement that made her hair bob. "Maybe just forget about it. I don't want to get anyone in trouble if they shouldn't be."

"And there was no one else around?"

"Not that I saw."

After that, it was time for a quick coffee break. As she walked towards Grounds for Divorce, she saw the museum sign out and nipped inside. She knew there was a big book inside that described the history behind the town's street names.

'Russell Street was named for a prominent family of Ledstow,' she read, with a sigh.

One simple sentence. It didn't seem like the author had done much research on the subject. Perhaps Esther could do better. She dropped a coin into the donation box on her way out to help with the upkeep of the medieval building and the purchase of more historical resources.

When she was sitting down with a hot coffee, she pulled out her phone and tapped some words into the search bar. Just one article about the history of Russell Street. She scanned it, quickly. It was named for the Russell family, who were wealthy factory owners. It sounded like they owned half the town at one point. There were a few protests in their factories about low pay. That was all.

After she got home, Esther made a list of the current suspects and their motives.

'Bettina', she wrote. A crime of passion? 'Lee', she added, underneath. They still had to check out his alibi. 'Cara,' she started writing. Then crossed it out. She wrote it again, in tiny letters.

CHAPTER 17

At the final rehearsal, emotions were high. The hall felt too small and people were sniping at each other.

Esther was having a bad day. It had started with her morning cup of tea as she stood by the window. The whole string and tag had slipped in to her cup, sinking to the bottom without so much as a bubble. She sighed, but couldn't be bothered grabbing a teaspoon, so she reached her fingers in to pick it out, not remembering that she'd forgotten to add any cold water to it. When she scalded her fingers, she jerked the cup and saucer and stepped back onto Louis' tail. He shot off into the other room and she screeched, which made Jay take flight from the windowsill, knocking the pot plant on her bookshelves, which wobbled for one long moment. It ended with tea and dirt on the carpet in her flat, both of the pets escaping from the chaos and Esther running late.

The fog was thick this morning, clinging to the fields with a bleak promise of rain. This was going to be a long day and she had started it by being late.

Bettina barely acknowledged when she arrived. Esther ran to her place. Bettina stepped outside, presumably to smoke, every ten minutes, but stayed in the doorway so that freezing cold air came into the hall. Lee stayed close to her.

Poppy told Roman that she wasn't interested in his collection of swords. Esther tripped over someone's leg on her way to her spot. Even Moran started the music too early for one of the songs.

"I'm sorry, everyone," he said.

"We'll forgive you, Moran," Bettina said.

Clark started his monologue, and Esther could see that he was determined to get it right. But Bettina interrupted him in the middle of the third line; not once, not twice, but three times.

"Lee, can you show him what I mean?" she asked, impatiently.

Lee took his place and delivered the whole monologue. By the end of it, even Esther was wiping a tear from her eye.

"Er. Well." Bettina said, at a loss for words.

"I think I speak for everyone when I say, give the man

the part," Clark said, and Esther privately thought he spoke with more feeling than he'd used to deliver the speech. "I'll do his role instead. But Lee deserves this."

"I think you're right," Bettina said. "For the good of the play. Will that be alright? You can manage that?"

Lee didn't say anything, but nodded, once. Esther thought he was overcome by emotion.

"Are you sure about that?" Esther asked Clark, afterwards, when they were walking home along the main street. The fog had dispersed a little but the air was thick with damp. She could feel it in her bones. "Giving up the role, I mean."

"It's the right thing to do, isn't it? And it's done now. I always felt terrible that Bettina gave me the role over him, anyway. Acting is all he's ever wanted to do."

"I think it was a lovely thing to do. And probably the right decision."

"Would you like to get some dinner? We should be able to find something hot at the twilight market."

"I'm starving. I don't think I've ever worked this hard at anything before," she laughed. "I really don't want to let anyone down."

The market was really just a cobbled lane closed off to the public, called Trader's Close. Colourful pennants were hanging between the buildings. Stalls on both sides sent a medley of smells towards them. Esther's stomach rumbled. Luckily, the sound of food sizzling and the vendors talking to their customers meant that it blended into the background noise.

"What shall we eat?"

They were drawn to a souvlaki stall by the scent of sizzling lamb, spices and mint yoghurt. They ate their dinner wandering up and down the alleyway, looking in at the hand-crafted goods. Mark from the cheese shop was there, standing up and stomping his feet to keep warm, and he waved to Esther. The ladies from the flower shop also had a stall, filled with brightly-coloured bouquets.

After they finished their food, Clark reached over and grabbed her hand.

"Are you sure we should be holding hands in public? It's pretty risqué," she said, laughing.

"No one's looking."

"I had the worst morning," she said, explaining what happened with her pets and why she was late.

"Why *do* you have a bird?" he asked. "And why do I feel like it hates me?"

"It's complicated," she said, feeling the first drops of rain hit her hand. "But the bird sort of helps me out. Emotionally."

"Okay, sure," he said. "Hopefully, your day is going a little better now."

"It is."

"Good." The clouds broke and the rain started in

earnest.

♫

AT THE DOOR to her flat, Clark was still holding her hand.

"Hey, don't worry about tomorrow. You're going to be great. I think everyone is going to be blown away by your voice," he said.

"Thanks. It's the acting and dancing and doing everything together at the same time that I'm most worried about."

She turned to unlock the door, then turned the light on. A flutter of wings told her that Jay had flown up to his normal perch. It looked as if the animals had been having a party in here while she was away. Well, there was time to worry about that, later.

She looked at him. "It's nice and warm in here. Come in, if you like. We can have a cup of tea. Or wine, I've got wine open in the fridge." She was babbling. She closed her mouth firmly.

He stepped inside, and closed the door behind him.

She took off her jacket deliberately, slowly, and hung it on the coat rack by the door. She could feel his eyes on her. She was wearing a cardigan underneath, which hugged her curves tightly and she trailed her fingers around the top of it, before beginning to undo the buttons. By all the bung notes in all the world, there were so many buttons.

It didn't matter, because he was suddenly in front of her, helping her, tugging at the buttons, sliding his fingers down to the next. He slowly pulled her camisole up and over her head.

He took a breath. "You're beautiful, Esther."

He took off his shirt in one smooth movement.

"You're not too bad, yourself," she said, as everything tightened at seeing his strong chest with a dusting of hair, broad shoulders and trim stomach.

Clark ran a hand down her arm and back up the side of her body, ever so slowly. His eyes became intense.

"Where are we going?"

She laughed, and pointed to behind him, then walked towards the bedroom, acutely aware of him following behind her and hoping she didn't trip on something. She didn't want to have to explain *that* to the paramedics. She suppressed a smirk. Surely, no one else thought these things.

She sat down on the bed and he advanced, pushing her but catching her at the same time so she landed safely and gently on the bed, with his mouth pressed on hers.

A LITTLE WHILE LATER, Esther lay back against the pillows, and Clark rested his head against her chest. She traced her fingers over the leopard sleeve tattoo on his right arm, that was at once so surprising and so natural for him.

"Can you tell me about this? I've wanted to ask you about it since I first saw it."

"Oh, this."

"Were you awfully drunk when you got it?"

"No, I was sober as a… judge," he said. "Sorry, no disrespect to Mrs Forte."

"None taken."

"I got it the day I turned eighteen. Used my savings from my first few pay packets. It's a design my mother painted, and she loved it. I took the whole painting, frame and all, into this tattoo parlour with me. The guy looked at me as if I was mad."

Esther laughed, imagining a young lad walking up to a tough tattoo artist with this huge, bulky picture.

"What was she like, your mum?"

"She was everything. I remember her as this vibrant woman who absolutely loved life, learning, doing different things. If she loved something, she'd sort of bubble over about it until everyone else ended up loving it too. TV shows, books, art, crafts, science, and especially history."

"She sounds awesome."

"She was." He shifted up the bed and put his arms behind his head.

"Are you hungry? I'm sort of hungry, again." She got up and drew her dressing gown around her. "Or maybe I'm just nervous about tomorrow."

"I could eat." He stayed lying on the bed and she drew her eyes over him, before turning to go to the kitchen.

She opened the fridge, humming to herself as she pulled out cheesy crackers, some beetroot relish and a half-eaten wheel of Brie.

Should they drink coffee or tea? Or should they have that wine she had mentioned before? Yes, she decided, looking at the clock. Nine o'clock was a great time for a glass of vino.

The wine bottle jiggled. That was the only way to explain it. She stared at the fridge door in horror as the bottle vibrated with energy then lifted up, very slowly. Leaping forward to hold it down, she gripped it as if it was a bucking beast.

"Getting started without me?" came a voice from behind her. "I heard you humming and thought that was really cute."

Had he seen it? Esther started panicking. Telekinesis was his specialty. He would be more than a little interested if he saw that.

"No no. I'll be there in a second."

"Alright, then."

When the footsteps receded, she gently let go of the bottle and it floated up until it was at her eye height. Just stayed there, floating.

She plucked it from the air and grabbed the neck firmly, ready to pour two glasses. This witchy stuff wasn't easy. She let out her breath, ready to be zen and calm, poured the wine and put the bottle away.

A flutter of wings let her know that Jay had followed her into the kitchen, and she realized she hadn't fed him or Louis tonight. She'd been a little busy.

"I'll get you some food," she said, reaching for the seed packets in the cupboard.

The blue jay hopped closer.

"Magic," it chirped. "Not too bad, yourself."

"Oh, be quiet," she said.

CHAPTER 18

The Cutting Theatre was buzzing on opening night. Excitement was high in the wings. Bettina had led a round of belly breathing, where she squatted right down, then lifted her arms up and pursed her lips to exhale.

"Legs apart, people," she called.

Esther was cold as usual and she stamped her feet in their boots to stay warm. She peeked out through the edge of the curtains to see if there were any people in the theatre. It looked almost half full.

Clark appeared next to her. He grabbed her hands and rubbed them between his. "Have I told you that I like you very much in that costume?"

"Like me?" she asked, innocently.

Clark took one hand off and lifted it up to caress the

back of her neck. He brought his face close to hers and whispered, "Want you. We never get much time to ourselves."

A shiver ran down her body. She turned her face to his and kissed him on his stubbly cheek. "Surely, we've got some time now."

He stepped in, pushing her back into the makeshift changing rooms, one hand fiddling at the neck of her dress which was, in fact, rather far below her neck, exposing her cleavage. "Don't write any cheques that you can't cash."

"Oh, my cheques never bounce," she said, smiling against his lips. "In fact, I have five hundred pounds in my savings account."

"No canoodling," Lee called, amusement in his voice. "Get in your places. Now."

They sprang apart like two naughty teenagers.

"We've had enough of that around here." Lee said.

"What do you mean?" Esther straightened her costume and moved into her place with a look at Clark, who was grinning at her.

"Oh, just that the understudies were always creeping around back here, thinking I couldn't see them."

"Right."

Greta and Freddy were only getting to know each other, weren't they? They were doing something very similar to what she and Clark were doing just then. But the way Lee put it made it sound more sinister.

Clark left her with a quick squeeze of the hand.

"Everybody should be in their places by now," Lee said, firmly, and made for his spot next to Bettina.

Everyone was supposed to be in their places. That was why the hairs on the back of Esther's neck prickled when she heard steps behind her. She listened hard and heard the soft whine and click as the back door opened and closed.

It was probably just Bettina having a cigarette, wasn't it? But she didn't think someone that committed to the play would miss the first moments of the opening night.

Esther followed through the door and rushed around the corner but the person was nowhere to be seen. She sighed and put her hood up as a few spots of rain dropped onto her face. The path between the building and the old gatehouse next door was deserted.

A piece of paper flew up off the ground in a gust of wind, and Esther ran to pick it up, doing her bit for the environment. As she got closer, it skittered further away again, but she finally managed to step on it. It was a handwritten note, with very small, cramped writing. A drop of rain fell on it so she shoved it into her pocket, before heading back into the theatre.

Lee met her at the door with a frown and a hissed,

"Get to your spot". She rushed to her spot and stood there, heart pounding.

The curtains opened and the lights glared and Lee stepped onto the stage as Orlando, in his wig, his voice strong and loud. Scottie came on from the other side as Oliver.

"Wilt thou lay hands on me, villain?"

There was a point at which you gave yourself over and became the character. It was like performing music, where the performer became the melody. You forgot yourself in that moment. Your own ego had to simply get out of the way and the song took over.

Esther thought she wasn't quite there yet with her acting, but she could see that some of the others were. Poppy, especially, gave an impressive performance.

After it was over and applause had given way to the clacking of chairs as people stood up, the cast trailed out into the foyer to shake hands and pose for selfies. Esther thought she could skip this part and head straight across to the dressing rooms, when Ashton came up and hung his arm around her shoulder.

"Oh, brava, Essie. You star," he said.

"Well done." Troy, Aria's fiancé, reached out to shake her hand.

"Don't crowd her," Aria said. "She'll be calling her bodyguard to throw us out."

"Never," she said, with a laugh. "It was nice of you to come."

"Are you kidding? We wouldn't miss it."

"Unless our favourite show was on," joked Ashton. "But I loved those modern songs mixed in with the Shakespearean lines."

"Just perfect," Aria agreed. "I think we've got a new favourite musical."

"A green and gilded snake," Ashton sang.

Esther smiled.

"Hope was here, too," Aria said. "She sat with us, but she had to go. She said to tell you that she was spellbound for the entire time."

"Your nan is way too cool for us," Ashton put in. "But you must be tired, Essie."

"I am. Well, I will be when I get home. And I've got to do this all week!"

She stayed for a drink with them, filling them in on what she'd learnt about the case.

LATER, while she was heating up some leftover pasta for a late dinner, she remembered the note and got it out to look at it. It was a little crumpled.

"'7pm dinner, around 8pm smoking, 9pm shower, Wednesdays football,'" she read. "Well, that's a little bit strange, Louis. What sort of a list includes when you'll have a smoke? Unless the person is planning on smoking fish or something?"

The cat stared at her from his perch on the arm of the couch, as if he knew exactly what the note was and she was of inferior intelligence. Or perhaps the idea of smoked fish reminded him of his empty bowl.

"It's coming, kitty." She threw the paper in the bin, before getting Louis his nighttime serving of biscuits. As she was putting the box away in the cupboard, Jay flew down and landed on the bench.

"And I can't forget you," she said, kindly, to the bird.

"Forget you," it chirped back at her. "Forget you. Forget you." It was getting louder each time. Obviously, Jay was still sore about last night's late dinner.

DURING THE DAY, Esther was asked to do another shift at her work. It was only until noon, and it would be useful to be able to earn money so that she could eat.

She was glad she had agreed to work, when Dot knocked on the door. Esther jumped up to hold the door so that Dot could wheel herself in.

"I'm so glad you came, Dot."

"I don't know you from a bar of soap but he trusts you," she said. "So I'm going to tell you what happened."

"Alright," Esther said, taking a seat behind the counter. "There aren't any customers right now." Blaine normally arrived at about 12:05, so they had about an hour.

"The booking was in Chase's name, and the credit card too. One night, I heard him arguing with someone, basically talking about attacking or killing another person. I sent that anonymous email to the police, knowing that if I mentioned paranormal activity, it would get to Clark."

She knew that was Clark's real job?

"Alright. What exactly did he say at the time?"

"'No, we have to get rid of him. An actor's death will send a message.' That's what I heard. I don't normally get involved in what my guests do, and I do hear a lot of secrets. But that one skipped out without paying, the little blighter. He deserves to get caught."

"So, you didn't dream of it, at all?" Clark would be disappointed at that. No precognition for him to research.

"No, I didn't. That was just to get your mate's atten-tion. There was another person in the room, I'm sure of it. I think it must have been his girlfriend. I never saw her as the door to their unit is external."

"You've been really helpful, Dot," she said.

"He threatened me," Dot said in reply, wheeling her chair around. "And no one threatens Dot Parker."

After her shift ended, Esther called Clark and told her about what Dot had said.

He groaned. "She was lying about the dream. Well, that's a massive pain in—"

"The armpit. Yes."

But Esther wasn't as disappointed as him. There was still one loose thread to be tied up. They needed to visit Bettina to confirm Lee's alibi. While they were there, they could question her too. By all accounts, Bettina was very close to Harding. She must know something about what had happened.

"How do you think this is going to go?" Esther asked Clark as they waited at the front door. "I'm not sure she's the type of person who likes unannounced visitors." The house was very large and the front garden was all white pebbles and hedges, trimmed and boxed to within an inch of their lives.

He grimaced, but at that moment the door was flung open and Bettina appeared, shirt half buttoned over a stained singlet and hair tumbling down. They had never seen her looking like that before.

"Oh, I'm happy to see you two," she said. "I've just saved somebody's life!"

Esther was used to the dramatic way Bettina spoke, so she simply followed her inside. Bettina didn't take their coats. She ushered them into her sitting room and opened the huge glass patio doors up wide, although the wind was freezing.

"Sit down. Sit down." She pulled a cigarette from somewhere and lit it with trembling fingers. Esther remembered that her husband was very against smoking, so much so that Lee had to meet her in the garden to supply her with cigarettes. This mustn't be an act, then.

"What happened?" Clark asked, taking a seat on a small sofa.

"The ambulance just left this moment," she said. "I'm surprised you didn't see it. The beginning, right. I was in the attic looking at some old papers when I heard Wendy calling out. She sometimes drops in and we chat about the old days. We have such fun." She stared into the distance for a moment. "I told her to hold on just a moment and that I'd be down directly, but she obviously tried to come up. I heard a little scream and so I looked down and she'd *fallen down*. That ladder is a rickety old thing that you wouldn't send your worst enemy up. I've always told my husband that we needed to replace it. And now the worst has happened."

Clark spoke first. "The worst? What happened to her?"

"She sprained her wrist!"

Esther and Clark looked at each other.

"Well, it could have been worse than that, surely," Clark said. "Sounds like she was lucky."

"The ambulance took a full fifteen minutes to get here. I hardly remember anything from that time, except that she was in a lot of pain. Oh, it's terrible for her, seeing as she just lost poor Harding as well."

"It was Harding's wife?"

Bettina threw Clark a look. "Yes, of course. Wendy. It's absolutely awful that she has sprained her wrist when she's got a new grandchild due any day now."

"Er, yes."

Esther cleared her throat. "Would you like me to make you a cup of tea?"

"Oh, never touch the stuff. Only black coffee for me and I couldn't possibly right now. I feel frankly sick."

"Alright."

"Forgive me," Bettina said, blowing out a long stream of smoke towards the door. "What were you two wanting? Because you've really made my life bearable again after those two quit! You're not quitting on me, are you? Please say that you aren't."

"No," Esther said quickly. "We just wanted to make sure you're alright after everything with Harding. You two have been friends for a long time?"

"Oh yes, you don't get to my age without meeting hundreds of people. Especially in the theatre, you know. You don't burn your bridges in the theatre world. You never know when that annoying person who played an extra will be your casting director for the next big production." She reached over and stubbed out the cigarette in a saucer then carried it to the kitchen.

Esther nodded. "Was your husband close to Harding as well?"

"My husband? Yes, John knew him, too. We were all good friends."

Bettina seemed to have calmed down a little by then, and she looked down and realised her top was buttoned askew. She carefully fixed it. "Don't look at me. I look absolutely dreadful."

"It's fine. Understandable." Esther rubbed her freezing hands together and looked politely away, out at the rain dripping off the eaves onto the garden.

Bettina closed the doors carefully, leaving a few centimetres opening for fresh air to get in and reached for a delicate bottle that was standing on the sideboard. A couple of sprays and the sweet smell of rosewater drowned out the smoke smell.

"Is that everything? I'm afraid I need to go and make myself presentable."

"One more thing. If you know where Lee was on the night of the 5th, could you tell us?"

"Lee?" She looked shocked. "How should I know?"

"That was the night of the big scream," Esther prompted.

"Oh, well. Yes, I remember that," she said, staring into the distance. "We were... practising when we heard that."

"Thank you," Clark said.

"I hope your day gets better from here."

"Yes, yes." It seemed as if she was trying to hurry them out now, so they stood up.

"We'll see you tomorrow."

"Good. Don't be late. Goodbye." The door closed with a click behind them.

"She is absolutely exhausting." Esther murmured, putting her hood up.

"I agree," Clark replied, setting off towards the car. "I wonder what her husband is like. He must have the patience of a saint."

At that moment, the crunch of gravel announced a blue car pulling into the driveway. A man stared out at them as he parked the car, then got out. He had long grey hair and was dressed in a red and white sports uniform, legs covered in mud, cuts and bruises. He was hauling a big red bag.

They waved awkwardly and walked out to the street.

"Looks like he takes it out on the other team," Esther whispered.

As she sat down in the front seat of the car, happy to get out of the rain, something was beginning to gel in her mind. A football player, the smell of smoke. The note! It had to be Bettina's note that she had found. But why on earth would she put it in writing that she was smoking when it was such a big secret?

Unless someone else was writing down her movements. But why?

"Ooh," she said out loud, as she plopped into the passenger seat, and pieces were falling into place in her mind.

"What's that?" Clark started up the car. "Are you thinking about Harding's wife falling down the ladder? I wonder if there was foul play involved."

She shook her head. "I found a note outside the hall the other day. It looked like a list, but I'm now thinking that it points to the killer being after Bettina next."

"Well, give it to me and I'll take it into the station."

"I can't," Esther said, panicked. "I threw it out. And the rubbish was taken this morning. You'll just have to trust me on it."

Clark tapped his fingers on the steering wheel. "Now that I think about it, I wonder... I wonder if there *was* something sinister behind Harding's wife falling down the ladder. If it wasn't an accident..."

"If so, whether it was meant for Bettina," she finished, and a feeling like lead dropped into her stomach.

"Yes." They both lapsed into silence.

CHAPTER 19

Before the next day's performance, Esther and Clark met outside the theatre. They were discussing in hushed voices around the side of the building, under the old weeping willows that leaned their branches towards the river. The rain had stopped overnight and the puddles had mostly dried up.

"I can't believe we were completely on the wrong track. Who wrote that note, then?" Clark said.

"Yeah, we have to keep Mrs V safe. What about—" Esther stopped. She really didn't want the killer to be this person. But it had to be.

Cara was in the area on the night in question. She'd been seen by Helen. Cara was lying about her broken leg for some reason. Had she been fighting with Harding that night when she supposedly fell off the stage?

But what was her motive? They knew that she'd asked to perform the play in the library. That would have brought a lot of new people in, sure. But it wasn't a motive.

"Caught." The voice came from behind them. It was low and menacing.

Esther turned around to see Bettina, one long finger stretched out towards them.

"Lee told me that you two are always hanging around together," she continued. "What is this? Some sort of investigation? Are you spying for another theatre company?"

Esther kept quiet and waited for Clark. She fought the urge to giggle that Ledstow had a rival drama society that would send spies into the play. That was a frankly ridiculous idea. If she looked at Clark now, she was sure she would burst out laughing.

"No. We are not spying for another production," he said, face perfectly straight.

"You're putting my play in jeopardy! It's already the unluckiest show ever." She reached out to tap on the trunk of the oak tree they were standing under in a superstitious ritual. "Touch wood."

"We think Harding was killed, Bettina."

The usually expressive hands dropped down to her sides. "Killed? By one of the cast? Why? How?" She asked quietly. "Do you suspect us?"

They glanced at each other, wondering how much to tell her. "Or one of the production team. We think that the killer might still be at large."

"And planning another murder," Clark said.

"Horrifying!" she exclaimed. "Oh, I can't believe it. I can't countenance it."

"We're keeping a close eye on some people who we think might be in danger. You're safe at the moment."

It took a few seconds for the implication to reach her, then the colour drained out of Bettina's face. "Me?"

"We think so."

"Where are the police?" she cried.

"I'm with the police," Clark said, gently. "I'm working on getting the case changed to a murder investigation. In the meantime, we have a few strong leads."

"Like who?"

At Clark's shake of the head, she started pacing.

"Me? They're after me? But we only have one more performance to go after tonight. Maybe we need to postpone it to another date. But no, the show must always go on!"

"We thought—"

"I shall stay away from the theatre. I'll get John to take me away to the townhouse. I don't want to bring any more bad luck to the play. We will finish on a high note. Even if I'm not there to see it."

"We think it's best if everyone continues exactly as

planned," Clark said, firmly. That way, the killer will let their guard down and we can be there to intercept their plan."

After a long pause, in which Bettina turned away from them and stared into the trees, she seemed to deflate. "Alright. If you think it's best."

"Can you think of any reason why someone would want to stop the show? Has anyone been angry at you? Was there anyone who protested at your other plays? Did you have any enemies?"

When she turned back, her face was paler than Clark's shirt. "Oh, doubtless hundreds," she said. "I speak the truth quite often, you see."

Esther wiggled her nose. She knew that the two main motives for murder were money and love. But it was unlikely that both Harding and Bettina had jilted the same person, wasn't it? So that left money.

"Wait, so the production was raising money for a charity, wasn't it?"

"Yes," Bettina said.

"What charity?"

"The Village Hall Society. You know, the old stonemason's hall where we were practising. They generously allow our club to practise in there for a very small fee. I thought it would be good to give back to them. They're doing up the hall."

"Alright," Esther said. "That makes sense. The drama

club would get the benefit of any improvements to the hall."

"Well, they do want to rip off the wall linings and make it warmer, which would be wonderful for us."

Esther nodded. "It's just…"

Something didn't quite add up. She knew that the murderer wanted to stop the show from going ahead. That was obvious to her, since Harding, the main actor, had been taken out of the picture and then Bettina, the glue that held the production all together, was the next target. But why did whoever it is want to stop the show?

"I suppose I should tell you then," Bettina started, "but…" She covered her mouth.

"What is it?"

"He was concerned. Harding, I mean. The day before he…" Her lip wobbled, then she took a shaky breath. "A young man was hanging around the hall. Harding got rid of him. But he came back later, when he was practising with Cara."

A young man who had probably vandalised the hall. Chase Russell. Esther was sure it must be him.

"Do you think that was what caused Cara to fall off the stage?"

Or was Cara working with him, a little voice asked, right at the back of her mind? She pushed it away.

"Perhaps. I should have told somebody," Bettina said. "Maybe he would still…"

"We can't look back," Esther said, gently.

"No," Bettina agreed, faintly, then after a while, her voice came stronger. "No, we can't."

♫

THE PERFORMANCE that evening went off without a hitch, although Bettina stood close to Clark, her face drawn. Later that night, Esther dialled Aria.

"Oh, hi, Essie. I'm just eating my tea. What's up?"

Esther opened up her laptop. "I'm looking up the charities register. You remember you told me to follow the money? Well, the play was raising money for the hall where the drama club practises."

"Okay."

Louis came over and carefully tested putting one paw onto the keyboard. Esther let out a long-suffering sigh. "I think the kitty can hear your voice."

"Is it my little baby? You give him a squeeze from me."

"He's right in the way," she said, as a pile of z's marched their way across the search bar.

She gently pushed Louis off, and he let out a little yowl.

"Don't be mean to him," Aria said.

"Right, Ledstow Village Hall Society. It says here that it's a charitable trust, and it was incorporated in 1924."

"Does that help at all?"

"Not really. Okay, there are six trustees; Langdon, Talltrees, hmm, Castle is in there."

"He's your man, isn't he?"

"Yes. That could be because he was their solicitor, though. I wonder if they have a website." She let out her breath. "It's so frustrating. Bettina reckons she has so many enemies she couldn't possibly say which one it might be. I think she gathers them around her like other people collect jewellery."

"Yeah, but it has to be a really special enemy to actually want to, you know, though. It seems like they hit her where it hurts. The play is her baby, right?" Aria asked. "Hey, lover."

"Hey, lover," Esther said, laughing.

"Troy just walked in. But if someone wanted to get back at Bettina, by ruining the production and her reputation, surely they would ruin the play on the opening night, not the last."

"Good point, Aria." She said, stung that she hadn't thought of that herself. "And they did try early on. Well, at least I think it's the same person."

"What if closing night has maximum impact?"

"Hmm. Ok, there is a website," she said, clicking through. "Proposed improvements. Heritage site. Lots of information about making the hall more sustainable. Nothing out of the ordinary at all."

On impulse, she searched for 'Chase Russell'. He just

kept popping up. An Instagram account with a few cricket pictures. That's it.

"I'm thinking that closing night has the most visibility, Esther. Be careful. Someone wants to make a point."

"Thanks, Aria. I'll let you go."

♫

THE NEXT MORNING, Esther felt herself growing ever more desperate. "Well, how about last time when I sang and everyone started telling the truth? Maybe I could do that again?" She was at her grandmother's nursing home again. She leaned back in the chair as her nan shook her head.

"It's too unpredictable, my love. You haven't done that one successfully since then, have you? And how are you going to work that into your performance?"

"Hmm, yeah. How did I even do that last time? It seems like it would be pretty strong magic."

"I've been thinking about that, too. I've got a lot of time for that sort of thing, you know. The conclusion I've come to is that, fortunately, those people wanted to tell the truth. It may have been something they were grappling with. Your magic helped the truth be revealed. You were able to do it because the change was small." She held her thumb and forefinger slightly apart.

"That makes sense. What about... Would it work if it

was a recording of my voice? If I played it quietly during intermission or something, I don't know."

Her nan frowned. "I'm afraid not. Although it would hit all the right notes, it doesn't have the magical intent behind it. That's why the song that all that fuss was about wouldn't have worked, unless one of us sang it."

"Oh, that's right. Well, my lovely nan, what would you do?"

Hope sighed. "I'm not a detective. All I can say from reading mystery novels is stick close to your main suspects. Soon enough, they'll let something slip."

Esther hoped that was true. They were running out of time.

Later, at home, Jay was acting strange again. The bird was standing on the bench, making his rasping noise, which reminded Esther of a donkey. Hee haw. Hee haw.

"I don't have time," she said. "Not now. I have to go out to the theatre soon. I've fed you. What more do you want?"

She got up to put her cup in the sink and noticed he was standing on a pile of papers; shiny circulars and some paper receipts she had taken out of her handbag.

"Get off there. I'll bin them," she said, putting her hand next to the pile, ready to push them off into the rubbish bin.

Jay squawked. He poked around in the pile, spreading the papers out.

"It's not nesting time, birdie," she said, amused. But Jay reached down with his beak and pulled out one of the papers.

It was the brochure that the bartender had given her.

"Ha," she said, unfolding it and smoothing it out. Her own face was looking back at her. There, next to her, was Clark. Beside him were Scottie, Poppy, Lee and the rest. But it was the names that caught her eye. She read it again and again to make sure. Her hand shook where she was holding the paper. At the bottom, in small writing, was a list of the cast. It clearly read, 'Poppy Russell'.

She rang Clark to tell him. "I don't know if she's married to Chase or what. But I've got a bad feeling about this."

"We have to question her," he said. "However she's related, she might have information about where he is."

"Agreed," Esther said, grimly.

CHAPTER 20

In the event, they didn't have time to question Poppy until five minutes before the show started. Bettina made sure they practised their scenes constantly, criticising every facial expression and crook of the hand until they were perfect, her face set in grim determination.

Poppy tapped Esther's shoulder, as they'd practised. It meant she was there, in place, ready to go. Esther's heart was beating out of her chest. *Poppy was tiny*, she told herself. Short and slender. There was no way she could hurt her.

"This is it," she murmured. The final show. And the final showdown. She swallowed. "Poppy, where's Chase? He needs to pay his debts."

Lee looked over, making sure they were all ready to

go on.

There was just a moment's pause, then Poppy responded. "I don't know," she said. "I haven't talked to my brother since he left."

Brother, hm.

Moran sat down at the piano, and played the opening chords. The curtain opened and Esther stepped into the lights. She moved to the left and slid to the right in the line of dancers. Then it was time for her first line of dialogue. She delivered her line, then paused for breath.

A long, high whistle split the quiet. She squinted into the crowd, recognising that whistle from backyard cricket games as a child. Right there, in the front row, was her brother. And there, her father. Next to him, hair newly done and primped to the nines, was her mother. Where did they come from?

She managed to keep it together for most of the play, keeping an eye on Poppy, who gave a moving performance. Esther's mind went into autopilot and her muscles remembered the movements and the notes.

As they started the duet, she harmonised with Poppy and they stared each other down, each trying to sing louder than the other.

This was the high point of the play, she realised. Her heart beat faster and she felt a little faint. Surely, now was the time for the murderer to come out of the woodwork.

The audience were captivated. No one moved in the seats. She tried to take a breath.

Just blooming well reveal yourself, she thought.

But the performance was flawless. There was an energy that transcended any of the other shows. Final night energy. Towards the end, Esther noticed dark hair slipping around the corner. Hmm. There was no reason for Cara to be over there in the wings. In fact, she should be on the other side, watching from where the rest of the crew were.

She frantically signed to Clark. She pointed to the left where Cara had gone, turning it into a dance move. He simply smiled at her, though, not realising what she meant.

The chorus joined in for the final dance. Her line was supposed to move towards the back as the other line filed across in front and stopped in position. She continued in the line and simply slipped out to the side. Surely, nobody would notice.

Clark followed her. "What's wrong? Do you need a jacket?" he asked, as she pulled the heavy door open.

It was cool outside and the sky was streaked in greys and purples. There was a faint smell of smoke on the air.

"No time for that. I saw Cara," she said, "heading out this way." She ran down the steps, looking left and right.

A roar of applause came from the windows. The play was over. It sounded as if people were stamping their feet. The audience's response was huge on the last night, and they'd missed the applause, but Esther didn't have time to wish she was inside.

As they rounded the corner where the other door was, they stepped into the pool of light, and noticed leaves shaking in the rhododendron bush. They glanced at each other and Clark went to look inside. Cara must be waiting in there for Bettina to come out, so she could attack her.

Clark stuck his head in and staggered back as someone rammed him. He caught their arms.

"What are you guys doing here?" Cara asked, annoyed, as she came out of the bush. She didn't sound especially guilty.

"Us? We are trying to protect Bettina."

But Cara turned to Esther with a curious expression. "From who?"

"From you," Clark said, exasperated with the back and forth.

"Ah no," she laughed. "I can see why you might think that. But you're on the wrong track."

"Well of course we think that," Esther said. "You were in the neighbourhood on the night that Harding died."

"Oh dear," she said, shaking herself free of Clark's grip. He stepped back a little but stayed on edge in case she made a run for it. "I didn't think anybody had seen me. Lottie will be grumpy with me."

"Lottie?" Clark asked. "The barista?"

They heard noises from behind the door and Cara changed to a fierce whisper. "This might be better discussed without him." She cocked her head at Clark.

"Whatever you've got to say can be said in front of him."

"Are you sure?" At Esther's nod, she said, "The Elders won't like this."

"Elders?" Clark asked, and Esther gestured to him to be quiet.

Cara sighed. "We've been seeing signs that there is someone in town who shouldn't be here. We do keep certain people out of town because of their history. Some of the Elders have their hands full so they sent me to find out who it is and get them out of here. And I'm almost there, so I'd appreciate it if you could just leave me to it. Please."

"And you think this person might be after Bettina?"

"Yes," Cara said, firmly.

"It's a bit dangerous for you to be going after them all by yourself, though." Clark said, with a frown. "A man has been killed."

Dangerous? For a minute, Esther was confused. Then she remembered that he didn't know that Cara was a powerful witch. She could see why he thought that she might not be able to defend herself.

"Someone's coming now," Cara said. "Quick! Get back in here."

The door began to open and Cara squashed them into the back of the bush. Esther had a twig scraping her ear, which tickled. She moved her head, slightly, rustling the leaves.

Bettina came out of the door, followed closely by Lee. "Goodnight. We've done such a great job," Bettina said, and turned to the right. "It's always worth it in the end, though it's often hard to see that on the way. I'll see you at the wrap party."

"See you soon." Lee looked side to side, before closing the door behind him.

Clark made a movement. Esther could understand the impulse to keep Bettina safe. She wanted to go out there herself.

"Not yet," Cara whispered.

Bettina looked very exposed wandering along the high street. The three crept along behind, Esther holding onto Clark's arm. Soon, Bettina turned down an alley. They heard a cutoff scream, then another, louder, one and ran around the corner. It was the street where the market had been. The decorations were still up.

Bettina was on the ground, covering her head. Something russet brown was on top of her. A fox. When it heard them, the fox sprang forward, and its lip peeled back in a snarl. It was between them and Bettina, and it didn't want to give up its prey.

It was a large fox, the largest Esther had ever seen. Clark moved to the right and forward; a small, almost subconscious, movement which put his body in the firing line. He was aiming to draw the fox away from Bettina.

Esther noticed that Cara wasn't there. She looked behind and side to side. A jolt of fear ran through her as she had a sudden thought that maybe this was a distraction and Cara had escaped them.

The fox bent down, ready to spring. Clark looked around him, as if searching for something to use as a weapon. Esther's pulse was pounding as she realized no one was coming to help. The fox bared its teeth.

Esther froze as the flash of recognition hit her. No one else was coming to save her. She had to use her magic, but nothing came into her mind. She chose the one spell she knew she had done on command.

She sang two notes; an unfinished chord, a breaking spell. And, just like the biscuit had done, the rope holding the pennant snapped and coloured flags and twine fell to the ground with a swoosh. The fox turned tail and was gone, silent as a shadow.

Esther breathed a sigh of relief, then took another breath, trying to calm her racing heart.

Clark turned to her. "Are you alright? We should buy

a lottery ticket, shouldn't we? It was lucky that the flag fell down." He looked at her closely. "Why did you sing?"

Esther was shaking. "Yeah, so lucky," she said, racking her brains for an explanation. "Well, it makes me feel brave." She trailed off.

He narrowed his eyes.

"Come on, Bettina, I'll take you back to the theatre," Clark said, holding out his arm for her to grasp. "Do you need to go to the doctor?"

"No, I'm fine," she said, for once not being dramatic. "A bruised hip and elbow is all it is. I'm very lucky."

"You are." Clark let her lean on him and walked her back towards the hall. "Are you coming, Esther?"

Back at the theatre a few minutes later, Esther went backstage to remove her makeup and get changed. When she came out, Clark was waiting with Bettina, who was reclining on a couch in the foyer. The audience had left, leaving snack wrappers and ticket stubs on the floor in their wake.

"Here she is! The production was absolutely fabulous," Bettina said, when she saw her. "But there was one real star of the show. I got a lot of comments about your singing. Some of them were from your mother at half time, mind you."

"I am sorry about that. Are you alright?"

"Oh, yes. I've been through worse in my sixty eight years." She flicked a hand in dismissal. "I have been thinking, though. Esther, would you consider joining us for another production? We're doing *Chicago* next."

Esther's spark for the stage had been ignited. Yes, she loved the excitement of live performance and the thrill of capturing the audience's attention and transporting them away for a few hours. The time spent and shared joy of a successful production made fast friendships.

But other people were a lot more passionate about acting than her. Others gave freely of their time and energy for the joy of putting on a play. She felt like a fraud. Here she was, a musician, taking the place of those who had dreamed of acting for their whole life.

And here Bettina was, thinking about the next show, when she'd just been attacked.

"Are you sure you don't want to take a break? You've been through a lot."

"The show must go on," she said, with a sigh. "I'm merely the vessel, through which inspiration pours."

"I notice you didn't ask *me* to join the next play," Clark asked, but he was grinning.

"You stick to your policing," Bettina said. She pointed to the double doors, where a man, who must be her husband, was approaching. "Here he comes. John used to come to every single play. Not so much, nowadays. Hello, sweetheart!"

After Bettina was picked up by her very shocked husband, Clark drove them to the hall. Esther explained what she thought had happened. "Can I just make sure I'm clear? You think that fox was Poppy?"

Esther recognised the glint of an academic in his eyes. *Oh no,* she thought. Next thing he'd have a clipboard out to take notes.

"I don't know the ins and outs," she said, carefully, applying lipstick in the mirror. "But I think a lot of people here in town might be more than what they seem. I just get that feeling."

"Yes," he said. "I think you're right. It just confirms that I've come to the right place."

Esther's heart dropped, as she realized he meant for his research. How could she ever tell him about her own magical identity now?

"I can't believe we were on the wrong track again."

"The wise man knows himself to be a fool," Clark quoted from the play, as he pulled into the hall carpark next to Cara's gold sedan. The old building looked spooky, lit up at night. He ran his hand through his hair. "But how on earth am I supposed to explain all of this down at the station?"

CHAPTER 21

By the time they got inside the wrap party, everyone was already there, including Cara. She was in a group with Bettina and her husband and Lee, who was doing impressions.

When Esther came in, a cocktail was thrust into her hand. "You made it," Helen said. "Everyone's talking about your performance tonight."

"In a good way or a bad way?" She took a sip of the fruity drink.

"Well, both, to be honest. Why did you leave?"

"Esther, you stole the show," Roman said.

She struggled to find a moment to herself, as people kept coming up to her. Clark was talking to Scottie, leaning against the doorframe to the kitchen.

Esther made up an excuse about needing to refill her

drink when she saw Cara heading to the bathroom. She waited outside, unable to believe everyone was carrying on as normal.

When the door opened, she said, "I've got a few questions for you. I know who that fox is."

It was in the eyes. Those quick, calculating eyes.

Cara let out a sigh. "Alright. It's Poppy."

She put her hands on her hips. "Thank you," she said, shocked that she had blurted it out like that. "But if she's still at large, why are we hanging around congratulating ourselves?"

"I've taken care of it, Esther. I snuck around behind and caught her when she ran away from you."

"Really? Why? I thought you'd left us."

"Firstly, because I thought she'd just run if she saw me. Secondly, because we never reveal our magic if we don't absolutely have to."

"But she almost attacked us!"

"I wouldn't have let that happen. It's just a flick of the wrist for me to stop her, but I had to wait for the right time. Too early and everything would be lost."

"Ok, fine. Can you tell me the whole story?"

"I'd seen Poppy hanging around Harding's house in fox form. I was following her, using spells to cover my scent, because foxes, like other dogs, see with their noses. Of course, that didn't stop me from being seen."

"Was that why you've been reading the book about wildlife?"

She nodded. "I had to learn everything I could about foxes," she said. "When Harding died, I had just nipped home to help my boyfriend. He's, ah, new to town and is still getting used to things here. Once I heard what happened to Harding, I obviously felt like it was my fault. So I've been following her around ever since. I knew she wouldn't want to disrupt her performance. I was waiting until after her monologue. She had been watching Bettina a lot lately, and I thought tonight might be the night. Turns out I was right. But how did you know?"

"That she would go after Bettina tonight? We didn't. And we definitely didn't know we were after a… fox. But we thought that whoever it was wanted to stop the play, and this is the final night. So it's their last chance. We also found a note with Bettina's movements on it. It was a little handwritten thing."

"That was mine," Cara said. "I knew I dropped it, and I came back to look for it. But you'd picked it up?"

"Yes. You can see why we suspected you," Esther said. "You looked really guilty."

"I suppose I can see that. But the coven told me to be sure not to reveal myself too early. That was something they drummed into me."

"The other reason that we suspected you was that you

weren't telling the truth about breaking your ankle. I realised, when I kicked your cast that day."

Cara rolled her eyes. "I did break my ankle. But it was magically healed that same day. I had to keep the cast on and keep hopping around to avoid awkward questions. It was a bit of a pain, really."

Esther's head whipped back. Magically healed? "Okay, that's really interesting. I better go back, but I'm going to ask you more about this. But wait, why didn't you perform the role in the play if your leg was alright?"

"Once I was given a timeline for healing by the doctors, that kept me out of the play. Then when you got the role and I was supposed to help you, it gave me a reason to be at the practises and keep an eye on Poppy. I struggled with myself about it, that's for sure. But I couldn't tell Mrs V that my leg was suddenly better."

"I suppose not," Esther said. It did feel that they had wasted a lot of time on the wrong track.

She went back over to Clark and watched Bettina get progressively funnier as she drunk more. She was a talented comic.

"Why is everyone being quiet?" she whispered, as the noise hushed.

Ashton walked in the door with his guitar.

"I messaged him to meet us here," Clark said, leaning in. "I thought you'd like to play some music for us."

"What do you feel like singing?" Ashton asked, grinning at her.

"*Jolene*," she answered. It was the first thing that popped into her head. "But I'm going to stay sitting down."

"Fair enough." He played the first chords as he picked his way around the furniture, then sat next to her.

Esther opened her mouth and let the music fill her up, feeling the pain and strength of the music. It flowed through her and out into the melody.

She looked around at everyone. Bettina had her hand on her chest. Cara's mouth was open.

"Maybe something more joyful?" Ash asked.

She nodded. They ended up playing music late into the night.

When her voice needed a rest, she sat back and simply listened as Ashton and Cara discussed politics.

Clark tapped her gently on the shoulder. "Are you ready to go?"

"I really am." She took Clark's arm.

Bettina flapped her hand at them as they were leaving. "You two. You had a hand in this. Meet Trevor," she continued. "He's the Chairman of the Village Hall Society. Tomorrow, we'll be presenting him with the profits from two weeks of a full house."

"Nice to meet you." Trevor was a slight man with one of those figures that are perpetually leaning forward, as if years of enthusiasm had transformed his body. "Thank you both so much. We really appreciate it." He pumped Esther's hand up and down with both of his. "The hall has been such an integral place for a lot of clubs and groups over the years."

"No problem at all, was it, Clark?"

He just snorted.

"You might want to join us at the working bee. We're getting stuck in next Sunday. Many hands make light work."

"We might just do that," Esther said.

few days later, Esther was walking down the main street, and noticed the lights were still on at Grounds for Divorce, although it was after six on a Tuesday. The door was propped open and the sign was still out. She slipped inside, wanting to talk to Lottie.

The chairs were all upside down on the tables. Light was coming from the kitchens. She heard Lottie's voice, and rapped softly on the counter, not wanting to give her a fright. The voice continued on.

"I can't help but feel like some of this is my fault," Lottie said. "I still can't believe we lost Mr Castle. He was really an innocent bystander in all this."

An older voice answered her, and Esther edged closer to the kitchen door. "Bah. That Poppy would have made it back in at some stage. She's been trying for years. Don't be too hard on yourself." It was Moran. "It's a shame about Castle, but we do everything we can for this town, you know that."

"I've been lax on the protection charms," Lottie answered, "and slow on the cleansing. I just can't afford to take my eye off the ball like that."

"You're really busy with your business."

"I mucked it up. The pixies got in and so did the Russells. Maybe I need to step back a bit."

"We've got a visitor, I think," Moran said, raising his voice. "My sixth sense is giving me a kick in the pants. Hello there?"

There was no point hiding. Esther stepped into the doorway, and looked from Lottie to Moran. "You knew about all of it?"

"Hello, love," Lottie said. "I wondered when you'd be coming to get some answers."

"We thought you'd be here yesterday."

"You knew that Poppy had it in for Harding and Bettina?"

Moran smiled at her impassively. Lottie went over to the chiller and opened it up, then emerged a second later with a bottle.

"Lemonade?"

Esther didn't answer, so Lottie poured three tall glasses of lemonade and passed them around.

"Right, well, she's one of the Russells. They're an old

family of fox shifters who have been trying to get back into town ever since I've been around."

"Long time," Moran put in.

"Did you know she was dangerous?" Esther pressed. She took a sip of the drink automatically, but the taste was something else. Lemon, lime and a hint of sweetness sparkled on her tongue.

"You like my new recipe?" Lottie asked. "The short answer is yes, but it is more complicated than that. The coven was warned of a premonition, and that's why Cara was tailing her. Pun intended."

"Who had the premonition?" she asked, determined not to be distracted by puns. "It was Helen, wasn't it?"

Lottie nodded, surprised. "I can see we'll have to keep a close eye on you."

"Do you want me to tell the whole story, lass?" Moran asked, but he didn't wait for Lottie to respond. "I can tell the story. Well, it was more than four score years ago. That's just how I start my tales, see, I don't usually count in those. We had a few more people in Ledstow back then. All sorts, there were. We had a family of fox shifters, the Russells, and we had rabbit shifters called the Brertons, and, of course, all the witches you could shake a broom at."

"And the Rhodes family."

He nodded. "Yes, the rat shifters. They were very generous people, and they did a lot for the town."

He paused for a second, and Esther nodded.

"A fellow named Collingwood got a bee in his bonnet that the village needed a hall, but some families weren't happy about it. Those families sent representatives down to the village to plead their case, but progress went on, nevertheless. Some of us wanted to have more of a conversation about it, but the Russells didn't think we needed a communal space at all."

Lottie leaned forward. "Can I add something? One thing you have to understand is that the Russells were employing people in their factories and paying them a pittance. They weren't very popular."

"At that time, it was when we'd just invited new people into town to bolster the numbers. We decided to keep the more magical aspects of town a secret."

"So the building of the hall went ahead. The forests around were cleared, I'm sorry to say. The foxes moved into town and so did the rabbit and rat shifters. But some people's pets got eaten and some chickens went missing and in the end, the foxes were made to leave. The Russells have mostly been fine since then, but a couple of the younger ones have taken up the fight again, especially towards our hall, and any efforts to do it up."

"So that's why it's always looked so shabby," Esther said.

"The hall is like a symbol for them, now. They have tried to block other efforts to do anything to the hall in the past," Lottie said. "Mostly harmless stuff, like protests. We didn't connect the dots in time. But, now, it's all making sense. We should have known."

"We should have. But we didn't," Moran said, comfortably. "Anyway, the Russells are one of the reasons we keep Ledstow under our protection."

"I wish you'd told me earlier about all this," Esther said. "It explains a few things."

"But you can see why we couldn't tell anyone why it was happening, once we realized?"

"It would be madness. Spoil the peace."

"Instead, you sent Cara after Poppy."

"Chase tried to vandalise the hall. We made him leave, and we thought it was all over. We did know that Poppy was staying with him. But we didn't think Poppy would be violent. Cara was watching her."

Lottie nodded. "We're all overworked in the coven," she said. "And none of us are getting any younger."

"Not without significant spellwork, anyway," Moran put in, with a wink.

"Where is Poppy now?"

"She's at Moran's house, under magical wards. We've got to decide what to do. She's killed someone, whether she meant to or not."

Moran nodded. "She's not saying much."

Most of the explanation added up. But something still

niggled at Esther's consciousness, like the sound of background music that she couldn't quite catch.

There weren't any claw or bite marks on the body. Harding's body was unscathed, and it seemed, to the pathologist, exactly like he'd had a heart-stopping fright. A heart attack. But he wasn't afraid of anything.

CHAPTER 23

Her phone vibrated, and she picked it up quickly, thinking it would be Clark. Too late, she realized it was her mother.

"Two hours! Two hours we drove to Ledstow to see you perform in a play. That you hadn't even told us about, I might add. We had to find out from Dennis from tennis, whose sister in law saw you on a brochure."

"Oh. Yeah, I'm really sorry," she said, stretching out her legs on her bed. "It was all really last minute."

"Your grandmother knew about the play too, so you must have had some warning. Then you left early, while the play was still going, so you didn't have to talk to us, afterwards. I know you saw us from up there."

"Well, that wasn't really what happened. There was a… situation."

"We were hoping to come to your flat afterwards to get a cup of tea."

"There was a wrap party on after the play. All of the cast are expected to go."

"Hmm," her mother said. "And you're dating a man, too. When are we going to meet him?"

Dating? This was out of left field. But, then again, her mother had always known these things.

"It's really early stages, mum."

"Have you met his parents?"

"I—" She couldn't exactly say that she had met his parents. It wasn't necessary, though. Her mother already knew, didn't she?

"You'll meet him, mum."

"When?"

"Soon. I don't know."

"Is he some sort of actor, then? Since you were in the play together?"

"Acting is not a guaranteed income," her dad put in.

"What? No, he's not an actor. Look, there's no drama. It's all very boring."

Esther realized something that had been bothering her for a while. There was no explanation of how Harding had actually died. She knew she was missing a clue, but what was it?

"Mum, dad. I've got to go. I'll see you both soon," she said, and hung up.

When she had said the word boring, it sparked something.

"That's because the crime is perfectly mundane," she said, light dawning in her eyes. She was sure that Poppy hadn't wanted to tell them all what had actually happened, because it wasn't a magical crime after all. She could be arrested by the Ledstow police.

She looked up ways of dying that looked like a fright.

"Broken heart syndrome," she read out to Louis, who was curled up on the bed next to her. "A rush of adrenaline may overwhelm the heart muscle. This can happen in cases of extreme stress, such as being told that a spouse had died. Ok, so it could be caused by a big medical event, but he didn't have any of those. I don't think something scared him. He just didn't scare that easily."

Scrolling down, Esther noticed an interesting article. Adrenaline, hmm. An epi-pen could deliver that jolt of epinephrine. She knew that Harding had an allergy, because Roman had told her that. Poppy had been a nurse, so she would have known exactly what the epinephrine could do, she thought, a chill running up her spine.

But if that was the murder weapon, how did Poppy know he had it? And how did she get her hands on it?

Esther grabbed her phone and pressed on a name to dial it. She happened to know of a parapsychological researcher turned policeman who would be extremely excited to interrogate a fox shifter.

"Clark," she said, when he answered. "This is your lucky day."

♫

"POPPY TOLD ME EVERYTHING," Clark said.

"Oh, good. What did she say?"

"Well, she only wanted to scare Harding off the play, at first. No big drawcard, no play, she thought. If he wasn't putting his name to it, it wouldn't be worth doing. So she started hanging around outside the house, pretending she was out jogging. She'd stop and talk to Harding but she wasn't sure how to approach the topic, so she just talked to him. His wife saw them chatting and, on impulse, he said that she was going to be helping him with his fitness."

"That night, Harding fought with his wife and she left. Then, when Poppy came over, he opened the door, as we know. He'd already seen Helen acting strange outside that night, remember."

"He had just given a large donation to The Village Hall Society. He said that to her. Poppy got annoyed and let slip that he shouldn't be supporting such a terrible cause."

He leaned forward. "As an aside, I think that Harding was more worried about his health than he admitted to his wife. I think he'd started giving away his money, thinking 'you can't take it with you'. Think of Scottie's restaurant, for example."

"Oh. But then why did he fight with his wife about his health? If he was really worried, too?"

"He was particular about things, shall we say? The costume lady told you about all his foibles. And we know he was a creature of habit and very stubborn. On some level, he accepted it. But he didn't want to do anything about it. He simply didn't want to change anything about his life at this late stage."

"I don't know anything about stubborn men, at all," Esther said, staring up into the air above Clark's head.

He cleared his throat. "Anyway, Harding and Wendy fought about his medicines. She decided she wasn't going to get him his new medicines when they expired if he wasn't going to look after his health. I think she was feeling desperate because she was worried about him. She left them out on the bench when she went to her sister's."

"As a reminder. And Poppy decided to stab him with an epi pen, because Harding knew that her brother was a shifter and it would only be a matter of time 'til he knew about her, too."

"How do you know that?"

"I think he must have seen Chase transform outside the hall. We know he wasn't usually afraid, but he was concerned enough to talk to his old friend, Bettina, about Chase."

"Right. Poppy must have put the medicines back in the cupboard afterwards. We dusted them for fingerprints and they're a match."

"So what happens to her now?"

"We can arrest her and she'll be processed like any other criminal. We'll pick Chase up, too."

She stared into the distance, thinking about how Poppy had acted. "Where has Poppy been living? Since she and Chase left the Gatehouse?"

"With Roman, I think."

"That makes sense. Poor Roman, though. He'll be heartbroken."

"He's young," he said, with a shrug.

In spite of everything, Esther was feeling lighter than she'd felt for weeks, now that the case was finished. She looked over at Clark.

"Aren't you glad I solved the whole thing for you?"

He frowned. "You wouldn't have got there unless I gave you all the information first."

"I don't know about that."

"Something really interesting that Poppy said was that she couldn't understand why she'd started to transform during the last song of the play. She felt it, like a rash all over, hot and itchy. She said it was lucky she was wearing the costume and so much makeup. She managed to make it outside just in time. Then she went after Bettina, running at full speed. Meaning to knock her over and scare her into stopping the show."

Esther shivered, as tiny feet crawled up her spine.

Poppy didn't mean to transform. She didn't want to transform. Esther had made it happen, when she wished for the murderer to reveal themselves while singing. One of her spells had worked, after all.

But how? It must have been such a small change, if Poppy was already going to transform after the show, a few minutes later. As small a change as a crack in a biscuit. How fortuitous.

Clark was staring at her and she realised her expression must be alarming. "Esther?"

"Uh, maybe she was starving? I'm not sure."

"Maybe. I just wish I could have a lot more time to research everything. A real fox shifter crossing my path, I can still hardly believe it. Now that it's a proper murder case, it's all rush rush. By the book. But I think I've got my research topic, at least."

CHAPTER 24

*E*sther was surprised to see Bettina pulling up floorboards when they arrived at the working bee. She was wearing a scarf around her head and leaning down to lever the plank up. She noticed them, and walked down the hall steps, wiping her hands on a pair of overalls. "You came."

"*You* came," Esther said. She never expected to see Bettina in overalls, getting involved in work like this and getting her hands dirty. She seemed calmer too, with a smooth brow and locks of hair falling softly around her face. Moran was painting the wall where some new shelves had been put in and he gave her a wave. Cara and her boyfriend, Abe, were sanding one of the windowsills.

"Well, I owe it to Harding. He made a donation to the hall in his will on top of the money from the play. He left instruc-

223

tions that a representative from each of the groups that use the hall come together to make a committee. So we're extending this part out and building a bigger stage. We'll be able to use this for our performances. It will be fantastic."

"It is going to look so good." Esther smiled. In some way, she felt that Harding had given a small gift to the lady who, she realized, had loved him from afar for so long. People to talk to, a project to focus on. That was beautiful.

"I never knew there was a handywoman hiding inside," Bettina said.

"I think we are all finding out new things about ourselves," Esther said. "And that's got to be good for us."

Bettina nodded. "You two can go outside, please. Check with Cara."

"I think we've been dismissed," Clark said, as they walked over to where Cara was in the front window.

"I'm glad that Lottie isn't here," Esther said. "I did think she would be."

"You just missed her," Cara said. "She went home for a nap. I think she's finally discovering that she is not superhuman."

Esther nodded. "We were told to check where you need us."

"Okay, we've got a really good number of people here. This town does come out in force when you need them, that's one good thing," Cara murmured, while checking a handwritten list. But, ah, we could do with some help over there." She waved to an extremely overgrown and prickly garden.

Clark set off for the patch and stood next to it, grim-faced.

"We should have seen that coming," Esther said. "We did accuse her of being a killer."

♫

"Do you ever get the feeling that we might be in over our heads?" she asked Clark, when they were pulling out the weeds outside to clear the area where the extension would be built.

"What?" His head popped up. Seeing him like this made her absurdly happy. He had his sleeves rolled halfway up and was wearing purple gardening gloves that he'd been given by Cara. The sun was struggling to come out, but the morning was warm enough, especially as it was hard work pulling weeds. "Why do you think that? There aren't too many thistles here. We'll be done by lunchtime."

He lifted up one of the offending plants and brandished it towards her.

"Not this," she said, wiping her face with the back of

her arm. "We were nearly attacked the other day. It was a close thing. Have you forgotten?" She knelt down.

Not to mention that the town is full of witches, shifters, and all manner of other creatures. Clark didn't know anything about Helen being a banshee. She left that part unsaid, as well as, of course, keeping her own magical abilities hidden.

"No, I haven't forgotten," he said, with a sigh. "I don't know what we would have done if those flags hadn't fallen and scared the fox away. Scared Poppy away."

"Exactly. It was very lucky." She smothered a smile, but a while later, she stood up, with her hands on her hips, watching him work. If you don't trust yourself, no one will trust you.

"I made the flags fall," she said. "I did it."

He kept working, but after a few seconds, he responded. "I thought so."

"I didn't know what else to do."

The calm response surprised her. But she realized that his whole background was researching this type of subject. He believed what his eyes told him. She was sure there would be more questions. But not today, at least.

"I didn't like you being in harm's way. We can take a step back from solving murders," he said, searching for a weed to target next. He looked up at her. "Maybe that would be a good idea. We take a break. No clues. Not even a cryptic crossword."

"Yes, I completely agree. The only problem is that you need the practise."

Clark lifted one brow. "Perhaps we'll get lucky, and there won't be any deaths any time soon. I can think of lots of other things we could be doing, anyway."

"Like what?" she asked, fluttering her lashes shamelessly.

He flung the weeds to one side and came in close, little leaves in his hair and all, and stopped an inch from her face, his arm resting casually on the wall above her. "Like listening to music. Watching Mamma Mia. Reading books," he said.

"I like it." He was trying to impress her and it was working. She pulled him in and kissed him thoroughly.

"That's enough, you two," Bettina said, popping her head out the window. "Get back to work. Today, all the town's a working bee."

THE END

A NOTE FROM K M JACKWAYS

HELLO! I hope you enjoyed Death and a Duet. I had a lot of fun writing this book and exploring the magical side of Ledstow. These characters will be appearing in Skipping a Beat, Book 3 in the Musical Mayhem series.

Many thanks to my wonderful beta readers and my lovely husband for reading and believing in this book. Their support keeps me writing.

If you liked Death and a Duet, please consider reviewing it on Amazon or Goodreads. Every review helps!

ABOUT THE AUTHOR

Kim Jackways is a freelance writer and mother, based in New Zealand. She loves shady green places and teaching animals to talk. Her stories detail imaginary worlds filled with magic, with main characters who are somehow smarter and funnier than her.